In Real Life

Ann O'Brien doesn't think much of Rose Kelly to begin with. She thinks she's silly, and shallow, and noisy. But things change: Rosie makes friends with Ann, who's lonely, and Ann falls for Rosie's brother Tony. She knows that he's got a girlfriend already, but then they split up – and Tony asks her out. In a dream, she goes to his house. What happens there makes the friendship between Ann and Rosie collapse, and leads the two into a tragedy that no one could have foreseen.

In Real Life

Anne Cassidy

Lions
An Imprint of HarperCollins*Publishers*

For Alice and Frank,
my mum and dad

First published in Lions Tracks 1993

Lions Tracks is an imprint of the Children's Division,
part of HarperCollins Publishers Ltd,
77/85 Fulham Palace Road, Hammersmith,
London W6 8JB

Copyright © Anne Cassidy 1993

The author asserts the moral right to be
identified as the author of this work.

ISBN 0 00674716/7

Set in Garamond and Optima
Printed and bound in Great Britain by
HarperCollins Manufacturing, Glasgow

PART ONE

The Death

It was a humid day when Rose Kelly was run over by a juggernaut. The brakes shrieked with temper and the huge wheels locked and dug themselves into the road until they came to a stop some thirty or forty yards on. After a few seconds, when the lorry seemed to shiver and shudder, a man got out of the cab and ran back. He stopped in the middle of the road and then, looking at a girl standing by the side of the road he said, "I didn't see her. She just ran out. I didn't see . . ."

He couldn't finish what he wanted to say and looked about helplessly. The road was empty, although in the distance he could see dozens of girls in blue uniforms running out of the gates of a nearby school towards him.

He put his hands over his eyes and began to sob, quietly at first, but then he turned and stole a look at the still body and his cries became loud and harsh.

There was no breeze as she lay to the side of the road, her arms and legs stretched out, her head at a crazy angle as though she were craning to look at some mark on her own shoulder. Her eyes were closed but her lips hung limply open, a small trickle of red and yellow oozing from the corner. The air was thick and hot; Rose Kelly's mother would've said it was the kind of day when you could have cut the air with a knife and fork.

Ann O'Brien took two or three steps backward away from the edge of the road, away from the weeping driver. Her eyes danced around, resting now on the body, now on the lorry and now on the driver. From the side she could hear the noise of running feet and a cacophony of voices.

She looked back along the road where the lorry had come from. She shook her head; neither of them had seen it; it had come out of nowhere.

The driver was wiping his eyes and his nose on his sleeve. She should go and offer him a hanky. Did she have a hanky? Avoiding looking back at Rosie, she started to search in her own pockets; her top blouse pocket, her skirt pocket, her other skirt pocket.

"I'm sorry," she said, her voice shaky. "I don't have a hanky."

And then she looked back at her friend. Her skirt was up at the side – any further and everyone would be able to see her pants.

She should go and straighten her up before anyone got here. She could at least pull her skirt down.

She took a couple of steps towards her and bent

over to pull her friend's skirt down. Her fingers touched Rose Kelly's warm leg.

"Rosie . . ." she said.

But Rose Kelly was dead.

The first two teachers out of the school were Kate Martin and Sister Michael. They wove through the running girls shouting, "Keep back, keep back. On the pavement, please, girls. Keep back."

They could see the stationary lorry just ahead, and with some elbowing they finally got through the circle of blue uniforms around the spreadeagled body.

They saw the driver, sitting on the pavement, his face in his hands. Ann O'Brien was standing, her face rigid, in her hand a navy blue shoe with a pointed heel. It was not the sort of shoe that was allowed in school, but the girls wore them anyway.

Kate Martin forced herself to look at the teenage girl on the ground and for a couple of seconds was rooted to a spot on the road a few feet away, unable to move closer, unable to look away.

Sister Michael was the first to pull herself together.

"You," she pointed at a nearby girl, "go back to the office. Tell them to call the police and an ambulance."

She walked across to Ann.

"Let me have that, Ann. You go with Miss Martin to the sick room."

The nun looked over to the teacher. "Miss Martin," she said sharply.

Kate Martin dragged her gaze away from the

body and swallowing the bile rising in her throat she walked across to the other girl.

A lot of the schoolgirls hung around as a couple of policemen pinned bits of white tape from lamp-post to tree to lamp-post and back again. Another policeman kept his back to the body as he directed drivers past on the other side of the road.

In the middle, two police cars were parked at crazy angles, their sirens silent but their lights swinging garishly round. An officer was kneeling on the ground near the lorry, measuring and making notes. Now and then he shook his pen furiously in the air, exhaled hot air onto the tip and continued to write.

A young policeman was helping the driver of the lorry into the back of a police car. "She just run out," the driver said, his voice still croaky.

"Just sit yourself down," the policeman said.

"I've got kids of my own . . ."

The ambulance men had see-through gloves on as they laid a long plastic bag on the ground beside the dead girl. One of them looked over at the half dozen stragglers still standing watching from beyond the white tape. He shook his head.

"Drunk, probably," he said, taking each of the dead girl's arms and laying them by her sides.

"Who was?" The other man's eyes followed the police car as it edged past the still lorry. His hands gently straightened the dead girl's legs.

"Ready? One, two . . ."

The men lifted the body a few inches into the air and then sideways; they lowered it with care, just as though it was a piece of fine china.

Two girls stood chewing slowly, watching the ambulance as it pulled away.

"That it then?" one said, heaving a large sigh.

The other, using her two fingers like a pair of tongs, lifted her chewing gum from her mouth and stuck it to the white tape in front of her.

"Come on," she said, and they walked off in the direction of the school.

At ten past nine the next day, dozens of rows of dark blue uniformed girls stood in the main hall, waiting for assembly. There was a general shuffling of feet and some nervous coughing. There were odd pockets of sniggering, but most of the girls just whispered to their friends.

Kate Martin took her usual seat on the stage. She nodded stiffly to some of the other staff and one or two of the nuns as they sat down. She picked up a prayer book and flicked through the pages. What selection of prayers would do Mrs Kelly any good this morning? The Hail Mary? The Our Father? Would these give her any comfort?

She put the book on the empty chair beside her. Perhaps they would, she thought with bitterness.

There was a sweeping hush coming over the girls, and, looking across the hall and into the corridors, she saw a number of floating black capes. She rose to her feet with the rest of the staff as the three nuns came up the middle of the hall, brushing various girls with the fabric of their habits, sending one or two into nervous giggles.

Normally Kate Martin would have glared at these girls, tried to reprimand them with the angle of her eyebrows. This morning she had no heart. After forcing Ann O'Brien into the ambulance she had no heart for anything.

"Good morning, girls." Sister Dominic looked round the hall. Within seconds there was absolute silence. "You will appreciate that this morning's assembly is a very special one indeed. I expect the best behaviour from you all today. We will start with one minute's silence for Rose Kelly."

There was quiet, and most girls lowered their heads when Sister Dominic continued,

"I want you particularly to think of Rose's family. Her mother, her father, her brothers and sisters."

Another brief silence followed, and some girls closed their eyes, but Sister Dominic's voice cut in again.

"Her parents will find comfort in the fact that they have been blessed with a large family. They will find solace in the fact that though God has seen fit to take Rose from them at this time and in this way they still have her brothers and sisters and in them they will see and feel Rose."

By this time most girls were wide-eyed and waiting for the next words. Looking round at her audience, Sister Dominic drew a long exasperated breath and said, "A minute's silence, I think I said."

Heads were lowered and eyes closed.

Kate Martin stared into space. She wondered if they had kept Ann in hospital overnight.

It was a strange business. Rose and Ann walking along one minute and Rose dead under a lorry the next. What on earth had made her walk out on to the road without looking? She remembered Ann O'Brien leaning over the sink in the sick room pushing her fingers down her throat, retching again and again. In the end she'd had to revert to what she'd seen in films and slap the girl's face. Not just once but twice. The first time she'd done it half-heartedly, not wanting to hurt the girl, but when it had had no effect she'd hit her the second time so hard that the palm of her hand had stung for minutes after.

"We will say a rosary." Sister Dominic fished a large, ugly set of black rosary beads from underneath her apron. An echo could be heard as the other nuns followed suit; there was a rustle and a sound like dozens of marbles hitting each other. One or two of the staff opened large black leather handbags and produced metal or mother of pearl cases in which sat small sets of rosaries, pink or green or white, sparkling under the electric stage lights.

"Let us pray. Our Father, who art in heaven . . ."

Kate Martin closed her eyes and tried to think of God. All she could see was a lorry, a crying man and a girl lying on the tarmac.

*　*　*

Ann O'Brien sat stiffly in the hospital bed. She had a small plastic tag round her wrist that said "O'Brien B1782". She was wearing a nightie that her mother had made for her, pink polyester with sharp white nylon lace round the neck, sleeves and bottom. The lace irritated her skin and she wanted to scratch. Instead she just sat, her hand limply in the firm grasp of her mother.

Maureen O'Brien sat on the bedside chair, her knees and ankles crossed neatly. She looked too young and too well presented to be anyone's mother. Her dark hair had been cut and permed into a fashionable style. Her eyebrows were lightly pencilled in, giving her a mildly puzzled expression at all times. Her eyelashes were lengthened with mascara and she had red lipstick on. She was wearing a dogtooth check, two-piece suit which she had made herself, red shoes and a small red handbag.

She hadn't looked like that when she came up to the hospital to see Ann the previous evening. Her face had been blotchy and her mascara had run. Ann lay on top of the covers of a day bed, sick to her stomach, and saw her mother walking towards her up the ward. For a moment she thought she was dreaming. What was her mother doing here? Hadn't she seen her leave with her suitcase that very afternoon?

Her mother cried when she saw her. She kept stroking Ann's arm and saying how terrible it had been, how lucky she was, how she'd always told her to be careful on the roads, how lorries were getting bigger and bigger and should be banned altogether.

She'd have been there sooner, she said, if she hadn't been caught in traffic around Euston.

And for a few minutes Ann had held on to her tightly, afraid to let her go.

This morning, though, Ann felt differently. Her relief at having her mother there was gone and had been replaced by anger. She looked at her mother's perfect make-up and her smart clothes with bitterness. Rosie was dead and her mother was still co-ordinating her wardrobe.

A policewoman had pulled the curtains partially around the bed.

"Now, Ann," she said gently. "How are you today? You're looking a bit better, I must say."

Ann said nothing.

The policewoman sat on a stool. "A terrible thing happened, Ann. Your close friend was killed in an accident. You were there. You saw what happened." Her voice was low and soft and contrasted with her black serge skirt and jacket and her sensible shoes. She wasn't what Ann had expected. Ann felt her mother's sharp fingers folded round hers. She could smell the scent of her mother's lacquer. She looked at the policewoman. Her hair didn't even look as though it had been combed.

There was a sudden squeak from the policewoman's shoulder and a small radio began to talk.

"Excuse me." The policewoman walked away from the bed.

"You'll be home tomorrow," her mother said, straightening the lace on the nightdress. She stopped for a minute, getting hold of a piece of loose thread.

13

Concentrating, her tongue curled round her front teeth, she snapped it off.

"I'm coming at ten to pick you up. I'm getting a taxi."

"What about Dad?"

"He's still at the Isle of Dogs. It's a bonus job. He's to finish it by this Friday. He says to tell you he'll be home as early as he can."

Ann looked down at the bed. Her dad had cried last night when he came to see her. Not like a kid all loud and with a red face, but he'd looked her over carefully as though making sure that some part of the accident hadn't hit her. He kept squeezing her arm and when he'd relaxed a bit she was sure there'd been tears in his eyes. Over and over he kept saying, "Poor Rosie".

"Now, Ann." The policewoman was tucking her radio into its place. "Where were we?"

The radio seemed just to sit in mid-air on the dark jacket. For a moment Ann wanted to smile. It looked like a huge ugly brooch. "What ave we 'ere then, a talking brooch?" she could hear the words, as though Rosie was there beside her taking the mick, trying to make her laugh in front of the policewoman.

"Poor Rosie." Her dad's words repeated themselves in her head. Turning to her mother she snatched her fingers away.

"You should have been here at the hospital when I arrived. You should have."

The policewoman looked from one to the other.

"Now Ann," she said, ignoring the outburst,

"Rose is dead. It was a terrible accident. You were unfortunate enough to see it. The thing you'd probably most like to do in the world is forget it. We'd all like to do that – not forget Rose, we never want to forget Rose. But we'd like to forget the dreadful accident – the way she died.

"The trouble is that we need to know exactly what happened; in case anyone was to blame. If Rose just ran out, without thinking, if she was playing with you and sort of fell back on to the road as the lorry came by, if it was a genuine accident then no one will be blamed.

"On the other hand, if Rose was trying to cross the road and the driver simply wasn't looking, or he was going too fast, well . . ."

Ann sat quiet.

"What happened when you were walking along Enfield Mount with Rose Kelly? What made Rose run out on to the road in front of the lorry?"

None of it made any sense. Rose didn't just run out and the driver wasn't going too fast, but how could she explain it? In the end, she would get the blame. Everyone would see it was her fault.

"I was here on my own for ages. No one came to the hospital for ages. Not you, not Dad, not no one." Ann said, ignoring the policewoman.

Maureen O'Brien's face looked troubled. For a few seconds she seemed much older, dark lines showing from the corners of her mouth to her nose. Then she smiled again.

"She's still too upset to talk about it," she said, reaching across for her daughter's hand.

The policewoman walked down the hospital corridor with Maureen O'Brien.

"I shouldn't worry too much. Shock is a funny thing. It hits people in different ways. It's probably best if I give her a few days and then try again. We really don't know what to do about the driver. It's so unusual, you see. We expect small kids to get run over, but not teenagers. They've got more sense . . ."

Maureen O'Brien waved to the policewoman and walked off towards the bus.

The ward was in darkness as Ann turned over in her bed once more. She had tried lying on her stomach, on her back, on her side, but none of it helped. Whatever she did, she would find herself looking into the darkness, her eyelids getting heavy and then something nagging in the back of her mind would make them spring open again.

She thought of Tony Kelly. Had he cried? Do brothers cry for their sisters? She didn't know. How could she?

And what would happen when they all found out that she hadn't been in school the previous day? She couldn't tell them where she'd been, what she'd been doing, why she had raced back to school at home time because she needed to talk to Rosie.

They would continue to ask her what had happened, how Rosie had fallen in front of the lorry. She couldn't tell them. She could not. But they would find it all out. They would.

Adults had the power to wheedle things out of you. Sometimes they were nice about it, getting your confidence, treating you like an equal. Other times they just thrust their sharp faces at you, intimidating you until you told it all, every detail, hanging youself with every phrase.

This time she couldn't tell. Whatever happened she couldn't tell.

She looked across the ward, wide awake. There was a small tent of light in the middle and she could see a nurse's head bent over a book or magazine.

Rosie's dead, she thought, and it's my fault.

She closed her eyes and pushed her face into the pillow.

CHAPTER ONE

It was just a year ago that Ann O'Brien and her parents moved from a flat in Tottenham to a house in Enfield. It was their very own house. It had a small garden in the front and a winding path from the gate to the front door. Along the path there were standard rose bushes. Maureen O'Brien immediately snipped a bud off and put it into a plastic cup she'd found on the drainer.

Ann followed her mother round from room to room, her footsteps echoing on the uneven floorboards, while her father waited impatiently out on the pavement for the removal men, looking at his watch and saying that he and Dermot could have moved them for nothing and that Maureen certainly knew how to spend his money.

As soon as they'd moved in, her mother started buying plants and her father started pulling out old cupboards and stripping off wallpaper.

"We'll restore these old fireplaces. I'll get these layers of paint off and expose the wood." Her father had a steel measuring tape and was drawing plans on the back of a piece of hardboard.

A couple of weeks later the bills started to come in.

"Rates and water rates!" Ann heard her father's voice.

"It's for the whole year, John. You don't get these every month. It's just the mortgage you get every month. I should get a part-time job again, anyway."

There was a crackle of a newspaper being opened, the pages roughly turned and refolded. There was silence as her father bored into the print with his eyes.

It was always the same when her mother brought up the subject of going back to work. Ann shrugged her shoulders. If they had problems, what about her?

When they'd first moved, she'd been excited about the prospect of living in a real house with a garden. When she'd visited Enfield, it was full of trees and there were older women riding bicycles with baskets on the front.

"It's like the country!" she'd said to her friends from the flats. "You can come up and stay weekends. It's only a couple of bus rides away."

At first they couldn't make it for various reasons. An aunt was coming from Ireland; there was a wedding in the next block; one of them got a Saturday job in "Alma's", the hairdressers up on the High Road.

Ann helped to unpack. She went on shopping

errands and walked round the local streets. She sunbathed. She even took the short bus ride to Enfield Mount to view her new school, St Theresa's.

About three weeks into the school holidays Ann took the bus down to Tottenham to see her friends.

"Look who's come all the way from the country!" one of them said. Ann laughed, but she was uneasy. "How's the gardening?" another said. She changed the subject and asked them about who they'd seen and what they'd done. They giggled and whispered and said that they were hanging around with a new crowd that she didn't know. There were boys involved, but whenever Ann asked for descriptions or information they just burst into laughter.

She had a couple of patterns to deliver to one of her mother's friends and on the way back she saw them all standing outside the sweet shop talking to a couple of boys on bikes. They waved, but she could see them nudging each other and pointing at her to the boys. She felt removed from them, estranged. Six weeks and they had developed a whole new history that didn't include her.

She wasn't really upset. She sat on the top of the bus on the way home, bit into a piece of chocolate and made plans. She'd finish off tidying up her room, maybe even consider decorating it (if there was enough money); she'd shop for her new school uniform and her school bag, she'd been promised a new pencil case and pen; she'd go to the local library and find out about youth clubs and maybe meet some new people; she'd start growing her hair – only this time she'd really persevere.

Storing her mental list away, she got off the bus a couple of stops early and walked through the back streets to the new house.

The evening of the next day Ann decided to put the first of her plans into operation. She sat among the boxes of old toys and books and pictures in her room and began to sort through them.

Most of these need to be thrown out, she thought, picking up a naked blonde doll and tipping out a set of "Happy Families" playing cards. She took them and some old books and comics and put them in a pile by the door.

A short time after she'd started, her mother came up and leaned casually against the door frame.

"Did you see any of the others? Patsy? Blonde Nell? Lil?" Her mother listed her old friends from the flats.

"No, I just gave Shirley's mum the patterns." Ann picked up an old annual. This definitely has to go, she thought.

Her mother looked fed up.

"Where's Dad?" Ann said.

"At work. Where else?" Her mother sighed. Since the bills had started coming in, her dad was doing overtime and weekend work.

"What about her next door? Mrs Wright." Ann had seen her mother talking across the back garden fence to an old white-haired woman.

"Don't talk to me about her! She wonders if my husband wouldn't mind parking his lorry outside our house and not theirs. Only it obscures her view of the street. She hopes I don't mind her asking."

It didn't look as though there was going to be much neighbourly feeling there. Ann flicked through the pages of the battered book in front of her.

When they'd lived in the flats, her mother was always busy. In the mornings she worked in the betting shop, and when Ann got home from school she would find her in someone else's flat, rolling their hair up or measuring them for a dress or a suit. She plucked eyebrows and bleached hair and helped carry furniture out on to the balcony while someone else pasted wallpaper and stirred tins of paint.

She talked incessantly about her friend's lives; Blonde Nell's brother who was a singer in a pub, or Lil's son who worked as a clerk in the City and thought he was someone. She was flushed and smiling and busy.

Some weeks before they moved there'd been a big row and she'd given her notice in at the betting shop.

In Enfield, now, she seemed bored and listless. They'd only been moved about six weeks and her mother seemed lost.

"I'm definitely throwing this away," Ann said gazing at a drawing of a girl in a tutu and ballet pumps, her long hair plaited over the top of her head.

"Do you want some help?" Her mother's voice brightened up. "We could put some of the pictures over on that blank wall over there. I could carry this rubbish down to the bin . . ."

Ann said nothing for a moment. She had wanted to do it on her own.

"We could have some tea and wee buns after. I've just made some."

Ann hadn't want to be palmed off with her mother. She wanted new friends.

"I'd sooner do it myself, Mum," and added, "if you don't mind." But her mother had turned heel and gone and she could hear her plodding down the stairs.

"Please yourself. Why don't you?" Her voice hung behind her on the landing and Ann added another dozen or so comics to the rubbish pile. After a few minutes indecision and guilt she shouted down the stairs,

"We could go down the market tomorrow if you like," but there was no answer, and she went back into her room, picked up the annual and, sidestepping boxes of toys and games, she sat on her bed and opened it to read.

They did go to the market the next day and the day after that they went to Wood Green and the day after to Cheshunt.

She hung her new uniform in her mother's wardrobe. One night she modelled it in front of her father. Navy blazer, skirt and cardigan; blue or black flat shoes, white plimsolls and navy blue knee-length pleated shorts for PE and games.

"Holy Moses!" he said when she came in with the shorts on." Is that so's they won't see your arse?"

"If Sister Dominic could hear you," her mother said, laughing.

CHAPTER TWO

At first, of all the girls that Ann mingled with at St Theresa's, the one she liked least was Rose Kelly.

Rose Kelly — Rosie, her best friend called her — was loud and overpowering. She was always talking in the back of the classroom and falling about, or walking backwards into people.

She was often in trouble and sometimes had to carry a Report Book around with her. She called the nuns "Batman and Robin", wore thick black mascara and had tights on under her knee socks. She rolled her skirt over at the waist and took her tie off as soon as school finished. Her blazer was too small for her and she carried her homework books in a carrier bag. Someone said she had a huge family and an older brother who went to a college at Wood Green. Someone else said that her brother went out with one of the sixth-formers at St Theresa's.

It wasn't that Ann was especially good (she'd been in a number of bad books in her other school) but since she had moved away from the flats she felt different, more grown up. She was no longer able to hang around the chip shop with a gang of friends playing those few games that had survived the transition from childhood to adolescence, Dares, Runouts or Bulldog; games that were played with a new excitement, that involved chases, touching, awkward hugs and embarrassed kisses.

There was no one to do these things with now, and when Ann saw girls in her school tearing around, involved in horseplay or making "shows" of themselves she felt at one remove from it. There weren't even any boys, so the games wouldn't have been the same anyway. She told herself she didn't really miss it, she had plenty to do. She went out with her mum a lot, and at other times she made plans about decorating her bedroom and did her homework. She'd even started reading some of her mother's books.

She was reading a book called *Love and the Captain*. She was careful not to let any of the nuns see the cover, which showed a busty woman in a low-cut crinoline-type dress, and a cavalier with his sword pointed at one of her breasts.

Ann felt particular irritation when she saw Rose Kelly lounging along the corridors whispering to her red-haired friend, her arm linked through the other girl's, their thoughts in some adventure that Rose was relating.

Once or twice she'd picked a seat in the dining hall near them or sat behind them in assembly and listened to their conversation. She told herself it

25

was only so that she could confirm how silly they both were.

Ann hadn't found it easy to make friends in her new school. She'd joined at the beginning of the fourth year and had been greeted by a couple of dozen pleasant girls in her form and had mixed with other girls in Options lessons and chatted to a few who habitually sat on the benches at the back of the playground.

She had people to talk to, to say "Hello" to, but it wasn't like having a real friend. No one saved her a seat as her form trudged round the school from classroom to classroom. No one waited for her in the morning to check off homework. No one made any arrangements to meet her at the weekend.

But she didn't consider herself lonely, far from it. She sat on the benches and looked at the different navy blue shapes and sizes as though she were an outsider; someone peering through the railings of the school.

One day, she took *Love and the Captain* out of her bag and settled into a corner of one of the benches to read. Rose and her red-haired friend went by, their arms tightly linked, both singing a song quietly. It was a song that had been on *Top of the Pops* the previous week. The words of it started to go through Ann's head and she felt a sadness and a longing to be singing it with somebody.

She let the tune play on in her head after they had passed and then looked back down at her book.

She threw a disdainful look after the two girls. Rose Kelly probably hadn't read an "adult" book in her life!

* * *

A couple of weeks later, Rose Kelly came and sat on Ann's bench in the playground, looked at the cover of *The Warrior's Woman* and said, "It's good, that. I read it ages ago."

Ann said "Oh?" and carried on reading. Rose Kelly continued to sit on the bench.

"My brother gets them. He goes to St John's. Have you read *Movietown Nights*?"

"No," Ann said casually. She hadn't even heard of it.

"It's about drugs and stuff and women who get to be actresses," Rose Kelly said. She was looking round at groups of girls playing rounders or "he".

Ann closed her book over and said, "Where's Fran?" Fran was Rose's best friend.

"In Ireland."

"Oh." Ann remembered that Fran had been taken to Ireland for a while by her parents. Someone said the family was going back home and someone else said that they were taking her out of Rose Kelly's influence, sending her to a strict convent school where they started lessons at seven thirty in the morning.

"When's she coming back?"

"Dunno," Rose said, and got up off the bench. "See you," she said, and walked off towards a group of younger girls

Ann watched her walk away. She sighed deeply and opened her book.

The next day they sat together in an English class. The seat beside Ann had been empty and Rose Kelly had stumbled in late and been told to sit there by Miss Martin. They were given a poetry book to share and some questions from the board to answer in their books. Ann had the crook of her arm round her book and every now and then she eyed Rose Kelly, who was intently concentrating on drawing the profile of a woman on the cover of her rough book. She pushed the poetry book towards her a couple of times but Rose, her elbow on the desk, her face resting in the palm of her hand, ignored it.

She was clearly depressed because her friend had gone.

She wasn't the only one who was depressed. Ann had no friends either.

Depression was a part of getting older. Ann had heard her mum say something like that the previous week.

In a way they were similar, Ann and Rose. Ann had left her friends and was lonely. Rose's friend had left her.

"I'm reading *The Dangerous City*," she whispered when Miss Martin was writing something on the blackboard.

"Yes?" Rose Kelly looked round. "Good?"

"Yes. It's my mum's. She said not to let my dad see that I was reading it. He says it's pornographic." Ann said it with pride. "I don't think it's that bad," she said, hoping Rose would think she had read worse.

"My brother's got some good books," Rose Kelly said, and she was about to go on but the bell interrupted her. "See you," she said to Ann and, rolling her rough book up and dragging her cardigan along the floor, she skipped ahead and was one of the first out of the classroom.

The next day Ann was sitting in her usual place on the bench, thinking about the coming weekend. Her mother wanted her to go up to Oxford Street and look at the clothes in the shops. Her mum liked to see the styles and then go to John Lewis and get patterns and make them up at home. They always had a Wimpy when they went out shopping, but Ann was fed up with the constant trudge up to the shops and back. She wished her mother had another friend she could go shopping with.

Rose Kelly sat down on the bench beside her. She handed Ann a brown paper bag that had something in it. A couple of girls called to her from across the playground, and she was up and gone before Ann had a chance to see what was in the bag. She took out a battered paperback book. On the cover were the words *Movietown Nights* in bold letters. Ann gently opened the cover. Inside in the top right hand corner were the words "Tony Kelly".

A sensation of pleasure fizzed inside her chest and she sat watching Rosie playing "Bulldog" on the other side of the playground.

CHAPTER THREE

It was the week before half term.

Ann waited in the queue outside the science lab. She was supposed to be saving a place for Rosie, who was coming from another lesson.

The lab door opened and a bespectacled face peered out of a black hood.

"You can come in, girls," Sister Michael said, and with a swirl of fabric disappeared back into the room. For a moment, Ann wondered why being a nun and wearing glasses always seemed to go together. Was it that defective eyesight went with holiness? Perhaps the kinds of deprivation the nuns were always saying they had to endure brought about a weakening of the eyes? It was one of the Great Mysteries, as Rosie called them.

Ann let the other girls file past her while she waited for Rosie. She was excited because inside her bag she'd got her mother's copy of *The Desires of the Rich*, a fat paperback with a beautiful woman on the cover and on the back words like "erotic", "sexy" and "sizzling".

Her mum had made her promise not to take it to school.

Ann felt some anguish remembering this, because altogether it made two promises to her mum that she would break that week. She'd said she would definitely go with her down to the flats on Saturday. As she'd said it, she'd known that Rosie and she were going swimming. It was better, though, not to admit the advance plan, better to let Saturday come and remember the arrangement at the last minute. There wouldn't be time for a fight and, as her mum would be going out with her dad in the evening, there wouldn't be such a long sulk.

Her mum would enjoy going to the flats on her own, anyway. She'd see her old friends again and catch up on all the gossip.

Looking up, Ann saw Rosie coming down the corridor. She hadn't noticed her at first because she was walking, not running. Ann smiled. Rosie was wearing a big blue jumper, the tiny blazer was gone and so was the thick mascara. She had white knee length socks on and underneath Ann could see the beige of her tights.

Looking down at her own legs, Ann saw the white of her socks against the tan of her tights. It was sensible really. When they got out of school they could take off their socks and then they didn't look so young. Loads of the girls did it.

It was another thing her mum didn't know about.

"Who's taking us?" Rosie said, pointing to the lab.

"Batman's off sick. Looks like it's Robin." Ann said, and they linked arms and walked in.

CHAPTER FOUR

It was late November, and Ann had been standing outside the Odeon for fifteen minutes. It was cold, and she was holding her two fingers up to her lips, taking deep breaths and then exhaling, her breath forming noticeable clouds in the air. It really did look as though she was smoking. She and Rosie had tried it once and Sister Michael had come swooping over to their end of the playground, ready to jump on them for smoking and had been as embarrassed as anything.

Ann wasn't sure if "embarrassed" was the right word to use for a nun. She was definitely put out.

Did nuns get embarrassed? Ann wondered idly. Probably not, because they didn't have the same feelings as ordinary women. Not that you could really call them "women" – after all those years of silence and prayers and eating bread and cheese their reproductive organs had dried up, so Rosie said. That was why they didn't wear bras and their chests always looked like flat blackboards.

It was only five o'clock but it was dark, and Ann strained her eyes in the direction of the bus stop to see if Rosie was among the group of people disembarking. She was not.

She fought off a feeling of growing irritation.

It usually gave Ann a warm feeling inside, thinking about Rosie. After being alone for weeks on end and thinking that she was going to go through the rest of her secondary school life as an outsider she had suddenly, from the most unexpected corner, found one of the best friends she had ever had.

After reading all the books they could get their hands on, she and Rosie would sit and talk about the characters in them. They'd discuss the things they did and ask each other what they would have done if they'd been in that position.

The stories they read always reminded Rosie about something that had happened to someone she knew, or her brother knew, or someone her mother knew. Ann sat open-mouthed as Rosie recounted tales of sex outside marriage and sex inside marriage. She told stories about her mother's brother's friend who had once been in the IRA and her father's brother in Belfast who had given up being a priest because he'd fallen in love with one of the teachers in the school.

After they'd talked and talked, Rosie would suddenly want to play a game of some sort. It wasn't a kid's game, Ann told herself, as she and Rosie dared each other to sneak in and out of the nun's sanctuary area or Ann sat on the bench with her eyes surreptitiously closed while Rosie found somewhere devastatingly cunning to hide. Once it had taken her twenty-two minutes to find her. She'd searched for most of the lunch hour, and finally found her in a confession box in the chapel.

When Ann had first started at the school this was the only side she'd seen of Rosie and she'd misunderstood, she'd thought that was all there was. But Rosie was like two different people, and that was what was so good. Ann could be grown up with her or she could be like a kid again. It was like having one foot in one camp and one foot in the other.

Thinking about spending time with her friend made her feel full of possibilities. Just going to the pictures filled her with anticipation. It might be that they just saw a good film, but Rosie had told her stories about times when she had gone to the pictures with her other friend Fran and what they had got up to. They'd pretended that they'd lost their ice cream money under the seats, evoking sympathy and donations from nearby adults. They'd sat beside courting couples and giggled or nudged every time they'd gone into a clinch. Once, Rosie told her, she had paid to go in and then waited till the lights went off and went down to the EXIT door by the screen and let her friend in for nothing.

Rosie was often talking about the things that she had done with her old friend. Once or twice Ann had felt some twinges of jealousy, but she'd covered it up by talking about her old friends down the flats and what they'd done. She'd boosted the stories up and exaggerated her closeness to one or two girls that she used to hang around with. Rosie didn't seem to notice, though, and was more interested in the stories than Ann's old friends.

Ann stood and gazed vacantly at the woman in the ticket booth. She looked at her watch in annoyance. The film show started at five fifteen.

She looked away from the brilliantly-lit foyer and out into the evening, her eyes taking a few seconds to get used to the dark. There were people walking along the other side of the road, but no buses that she could see. She stamped her feet on the pavement to keep out the cold. The trouble was that Rosie wasn't always on time and twice she hadn't even turned up when they'd arranged to meet.

Ann stood agitatedly on the pavement. Looking down, she caught sight of her new boots. They were black leather, and she'd bought them the previous day.

Rosie had had a good excuse each time she hadn't turned up, and Ann hadn't been able to keep her anger up for more than a few minutes. Her dad hadn't any change to give her money for the buses; there was no one to look after the baby while her mum went to evening mass.

Ann held her foot out to the side so that she could get a profile of the boot and its heel. She bristled with pride. One good thing about having no brothers and sisters was that when there was money going you got it spent on you.

She'd worried at first that Rosie might mind; that the fact that Ann had new boots or a new coat or the money for the pictures might bother Rosie. But she never really seemed to notice. She let Ann pay for things without any comment and praised Ann's clothes without any jealousy. She'd say, "I like those shoes, they're smashing." or, "Got any cash? Get us a Flake," without any qualms.

And Ann didn't mind. She had money, so why not? Rosie had a big family, so she didn't. It was as she said to her mum one day,

"It's not as though Rosie's got the money and just isn't paying her way."

Her mum had just pursed her lips.

Her mum hadn't met Rosie, but she didn't like her. She said her accent on the phone was common and if Ann was late home from school or couldn't go somewhere with her, she blamed it on The Fabulous Rose Kelly.

Rosie could have rung, though. Each time she hadn't turned up she could have picked up a phone, dialled her number and said she wasn't going to come.

It was twenty past five. Rosie was half an hour late. Ann knew she wasn't coming. Using her new boot, she kicked at a discarded wrapper on the pavement.

A bus stopped just as she was about to walk off and two teenagers got off, a boy and a girl, linking arms.

They walked towards her intently. She noticed the boy's leather jacket immediately. The girl was much shorter, balancing on high-heeled shoes. She also had a leather jacket on and a short straight skirt. Her knees looked bony and seemed to hit each other as she walked and as she came closer there was a scraping sound as she dragged the heels of her shoes along the pavement. Her face looked familiar, although Ann couldn't place her.

"You Ann?" The boy said. He was about seventeen. His hair was cut very short and his skin was pale.

"Yes," she said, not sure of what was happening.

"Tony," he said, not looking at her. "Tony Kelly."

He took a packet of Wrigleys out of his pocket, undid one, and then pushed it slowly into his mouth. His eyes rested on the departing bus and he seemed to follow it until it disappeared into the darkness.

"Want one, Pat?" he said.

Ann looked him over: his clothes, his hair, the gold of a thin chain round his neck. It was Tony Kelly, Rosie's brother.

Her eyes were drawn to the black leather sleeve that was linked through his arm, and she came face to face with the blonde girl who was also sliding a piece of gum into her mouth. The girl was gazing at the film poster, ignoring her completely, and Ann noticed how her eyes were elaborately made up; she had black lines and dark eye shadow on the lids and, standing straight out like two small paintbrushes, were false eyelashes.

It was Patricia Hogan, a sixth-former from her school, the one that Rosie had pointed out in assembly who went out with her brother.

"Rosie can't come," Tony Kelly finally said. "Me mum's got to go over her sister's. Rosie's looking after the baby. I was coming here anyroad so I said I'd tell you."

The girl looked cold, her arms visibly shivering. The leather jacket was hanging open, and underneath Ann thought she could see a thin V-necked T-shirt.

"All right?" he said, looking straight at her for a moment.

"Yes," Ann said, and his face broke into a broad smile. She smiled back, looking from Rosie's brother to his girlfriend. Patricia Hogan's face was blank, as though she was looking through Ann into the dark street beyond. Without another word, they turned round and, in a stately manner, walked towards the light and warmth of the cinema.

Confused, Ann started to walk towards the bus stop. That was Rosie's elder brother! She hadn't pictured him like that at all. He went to St John's College at Wood Green. She'd seen some of those boys at a special mass one day last half term. She'd pictured a skinny lad in a brown and yellow blazer peering through unfashionable black glasses at a paperback book, looking furtively round in case his parents or the teachers at school caught him. Tony Kelly with a shelf of dirty books!

And Patricia, pale and skinny in school; out of school, her black eyes and her long legs made her look about twenty.

Ann's bus came within minutes and she got on. She sat looking at her new leather boots and felt dissatisfied with herself. She would have bought high-heeled shoes if she hadn't had her mum standing over her in the shop. She'd wear heavy eye make-up like that if her mum didn't inspect her every time she walked out of the front door. And Patricia was so small; the word "petite" jumped into Ann's head and she felt large and cumbersome on the bus seat.

Into her head came the warm smile that Tony Kelly had shown her. She smiled and looked at her reflection in the bus window. That was what he had seen. What had he thought?

She went over the brief conversation outside the cinema. I should have said something more than yes, she thought. I could have made conversation, asked them what they were going to see.

Standing up for her stop, she thought about going home. Her mother would know something was wrong when she got back so early. In the end she would find out that Rosie had let her down and would add it to her list of Reasons Why Rosie Was Not A Good Friend.

But Rosie had sent her brother to tell Ann she wasn't coming.

Going through the front door, she saw her mother leaning against the living-room doorframe in almost exactly the same place she had been when Ann went out. Ann didn't speak. She knew she didn't have to.

"I knew you'd be back early," her mother said.

She didn't bother to answer and went straight up to her bedroom, put some music on and thought about Tony Kelly.

PART TWO

The Funeral

Along Enfield Mount and down Spring Hill was a never-ending line of navy blue blazers. Kate Martin was leading a third-year class and found herself in the ridiculous position of standing like a lollipop lady in the middle of every road they crossed and then sprinting past them in order to get to the front before they reached the next one.

Once or twice she nearly bumped into Sister Dominic, who was briskly zig-zagging through the girls, checking uniforms and make-up. Every now and then the nun grabbed the sleeve of a blazer and tutting loudly, added a name to a mental black book, and sent a red-faced girl to the back of the long procession.

The funeral had been arranged for the first Monday of the summer holidays, and Kate Martin had been involved in the frantic duplicating of letters to parents urging them to make sure their daughters were in the school playground at nine thirty in full school uniform. It was a lot to ask, but the death of a teenage girl had sent ripples of apprehension through the other parents. They'd given generously to collections for flowers and mass cards. Letters had been written and cards had been sent, instructions to daughters had been restated; come straight home from school, don't play silly games on the streets, be careful on the roads.

Watching the girls filing in through the giant wooden doors of the church, Kate calculated that most of them had made it. One or two had come tearfully to the staffroom on the last day of term and in the usual exaggerated manner had declared that they would do anything to get out of their holiday to France or Cornwall or Ireland, anything. Kate had told them that it was all right and one or two had proclaimed that they would say a rosary every day of the summer holidays for Rose Kelly.

In the church, Kate sat among the sixth-formers, at the end of a row near the back. In the far distance, through the gloom of the huge church, she could see the variegated shades of blue or black worn by the close members of the family. Between her and them was row on row of navy shoulders and mousy heads, brightened only by flashes of blonde or red hair which stood out against the grey stone interior.

Kate wondered if Ann O'Brien was up at the front with the family. A couple of rows in front of her she saw Patricia Hogan, her head bent as if in prayer. One of the other teachers had said that she was the older brother's girlfriend.

Kate found her gaze resting uncomfortably on the wooden box far away up at the front standing on four legs, a profusion of colour on the top from the flowers placed there.

She looked round to make sure there was no giggling or silliness. She smiled because it occurred to her that the one person she would have had to reprimand in this situation was Rose Kelly. Skinny Rose, who always had a cheeky comment or a risqué suggestion.

Are you married, Miss? Why not, Miss? Don't you like men, Miss? Are you going to be a nun, Miss? I saw you getting out of a man's car, Miss. Is he your husband, Miss? Is that ring an engagement ring, Miss? Are you ever going to get married, Miss?

Kate remembered gazing idly out of the staffroom window one day and seeing Rose Kelly leaping in and out of a skipping game, causing outrage among first-years. A few minutes later, just after the bell from registration had gone, she'd walked into one of the toilets and found Rose applying mascara to her eyelashes.

Not quite grown up and not quite a child, Kate thought. People began to rise to their feet around her, and in the distance she saw the priest and the altar boys come out of the vestry.

It was about three weeks since the accident. There had been an inquest, and Kate had gone along with Sister Dominic and some of the other nuns.

The driver had been wearing a dark suit and white shirt. When he was being questioned he had

42

his hands loosely clasped, but every now and then he pulled them apart agitatedly and held on to the wooden rest in front of him as though gripping some invisible steering wheel.

No, he had not seen the girl, she had just appeared out of nowhere. Yes, he'd noticed numbers of schoolgirls walking along Enfield Mount and then suddenly there was this one hurtling out onto the road in front of him. No, there had been no time to stop; one minute the road was clear the next she was there. He had no memory of her face or her hair or her expression. She was just a navy blue shape that came from nowhere. The driver had faltered, his voice breaking. He'd let go of the "steering wheel", searched his pockets and brought out a white handkerchief.

No, he hadn't been drinking. He never took a drop when he was working. Yes, he had been driving for a couple of hours but he wasn't tired, far from it.

He had nothing to add except that he had been driving for fifteen years. He hadn't made so much as a scratch on his cab; his licence was clean; his record unblemished. No, he would never forget that day; every time he looked at his daughter and his son he would think of that young girl lying on the road.

A woman who lived across the road from the accident had been on the phone to her friend at the time. No, she hadn't actually been looking out of the window, rather just gazing through it as she was chatting to her friend (not a *friend* actually, more of an acquaintance). She had only noticed the two girls at all because for a minute or two before the lorry went by they seemed to be playing some game where they were both holding hands and swinging around. She'd kept looking because at the time she'd thought it was odd that girls of that age should play games at all.

No, she hadn't seen Rose Kelly go onto the road. It had all happened so quickly and she had been talking to her friend on the phone. One minute she saw the girls playing and the next she'd heard the terrible screech of the lorry's brakes.

No, she hadn't run out. She'd put the phone down and dialled 999. She hadn't been able to see the body herself but she'd known from the way the driver and other people were running towards it that someone had got run over. No, she was sorry, she hadn't seen more. She really couldn't say if the driver had been going too fast, she didn't drive herself and couldn't judge. It seemed to her that all cars went too fast these days anyway.

The policeman showed a diagram of the position of the body and gave measurements of the wheel marks made by the lorry. No, in his opinion the driver had not been going too fast. Yes, there were cars parked on that side of the road but there were only three or four and they were not close enough to obscure the view of a person of average height. Yes, it was true that Rose Kelly's schoolbag had been found on the pavement. This suggested to him that she hadn't been planning to cross the road at all but had put it down with the intention of retrieving it later.

The pathologist had a pink carnation in his lapel and spoke crisply, starting his answers just before the coroner had finished his questions. The body had sustained multiple bruising and some broken bones. There was internal bleeding and the spine had been severed. The injuries were concurrent with a blow, probably caused by the impact with the lorry and the ground. Actual death was caused by a broken neck.

Ann O'Brien's answers were quiet and tearful. No, they hadn't been playing dares. No, they hadn't been messing around. She couldn't remember exactly what they had been doing just before the accident. She thought they were talking. It wasn't exactly an argument, more like a discussion. She thought Rosie was going to cross the road. No, she couldn't explain why Rosie had left her bag on the pavement, it had all happened so quickly. Yes, she supposed Rosie was a mischievous girl. Yes, she didn't always think carefully about what she was doing. Yes, it was possible that she just thoughtlessly stepped out onto the road. It was possible, but Ann O'Brien couldn't remember if that was what happened.

Kate Martin had watched as the court clerk had handed Ann a box of tissues.

The coroner's face was impassive when he summed up. It was a tragedy. It was inexplicable why a teenage girl had careered onto the road like a toddler. It had to be a consolation to the parents that she wouldn't have known anything; she wouldn't have felt any pain or had any knowledge of what had happened to her. His verdict was Accidental Death.

The congregation sat down for the sermon. Amid coughs and the scraping of chairs, Kate wondered what had happened to the beginning of the mass. She had been preoccupied with her own thoughts instead of paying attention.

The priest cleared his throat a couple of times, looked at the coffin and then towards the pews where the family were sitting.

"Nothing saddens me more than speaking to a family about losing a child. In some way or other it is my duty to say to that family that this death, this taking of your loved one, this untimely exit – this is part of God's plan.

"We want to cry out and say 'Why us? Why our daughter? What part of God's blueprint could involve our Rose?'"

Kate looked around. She had heard this sort of thing at funerals before. She felt a mild irritation towards the man. Had he gone to a book that morning and chosen a sermon for a dead fifteen-year-old girl? Were there books in the vestry that had different chapters for the deaths of mothers, fathers, friends, babies?

She bit her lip. It wasn't the priest's fault that Rose was dead. His words went over her head as she looked at some of the girls around her. *Journey through life . . . Son of God . . . precious love of parents . . . lost youth . . .*

One or two girls had their eyes fastened on the priest, but most seemed to be staring absent-mindedly. *Eternal love . . . life after death . . . always remember . . .*

Patricia Hogan was painstakingly picking bits of fluff off the sleeve of her blazer. *Virgin Mary . . . Rose Kelly . . . reunited . . . have faith in God . . .*

Kate looked up to the front of the church. For a brief moment the coffin looked like the wooden horse that the girls jumped over in PE. Then, in a moment, it was a coffin again.

"Let us pray." The priest had finished his sermon. Kate bowed her head.

The coffin was carried down the aisle by Rose's father, her older brother and some of the under-taker's men. On top, the colourful wreath made up the letters ROSE in red, pink, white and green.

Behind it, in slow procession, walked Rose's mother and her younger sisters and brothers.

At the back were friends of the family and in the middle, with her parents, was Ann O'Brien, her head bowed.

Ann O'Brien looked up as she passed, and Kate noticed her eyes darting about. She seemed to look straight at her and then away towards Patricia Hogan, then back to the mourner in front then back to Kate. The other mourners' expressions were glazed, a bit drunk looking, their lips pushing together, their skin colour heightened, red blotches on their cheeks. Ann O'Brien's mouth was rigidly slightly open, a dark shape on a pale face.

Rose Kelly's mourners looked tired, listless, as though they had done a lot of work that had led to nothing.

Ann O'Brien looked jumpy, apprehensive.

Afterwards, as Kate watched the black cars glide

away from the front of the church, she thought about the expression on Ann O'Brien's face.

Ann O'Brien was afraid of something.

It was overcast in the cemetery, and Ann O'Brien stood tightly wedged between her mother and father some two or three rows back from the grave.

The casket was being lowered; Ann looked at it in a detached way. Inside that box Rosie was lying. She was wearing her school uniform, someone had said.

For a few seconds Ann wanted to laugh out loud. Rosie in that box in a blue cardigan, skirt, white shirt, tie, knee-length white socks and black shoes. If it had been someone else she could have let her mouth open wide and roar with glee. It was probably the only time Rosie had worn the correct school uniform, the only time ever.

Nagging feelings of guilt began to settle on her chest. She coughed, but it was dry and unnecessary.

She looked round the cemetery at the graves, the green lawns and the gravel paths that ran between them.

In the daylight it looked like a park. There were a couple of benches along by the road and a few flower beds. Some of the graves had small potted plants on them, and painted stone figures that were probably meant to be saints.

She thought about what it would be like at night. There were no lights that she could see; it would be pitch dark. If it was windy the bushes would move about eerily and the branches on the trees would creek and shudder. In her mind she saw a black sky and a yellow flash of lightning; she saw the grave stones like giant crooked teeth in a dark cavernous mouth and the statuettes staring into the driving rain, their eyes glinting.

Rosie would have to lie there through it all. She'd be flat on her back in her blue cardigan and skirt and her blue and white striped tie. All around the box there would be dirt ("earth", everyone else called it), underneath, at the side, on top of the lid; shovelfuls of black dirt.

Ann could feel her parents' elbows on each side of her and she slipped her hand through her dad's arm. Her mother leaned across and whispered something that she couldn't hear and her dad gave a curt nod.

She looked at her dad who was staring in the direction of the priest.

Had he known how close her mum had been to leaving him? Had he known that she had taken the brown suitcase and walked out of the front door never to come back?

He didn't know. He hadn't seen her. Only Ann had seen her step out of the front gate, her cream dress and red shoes, her hair glowing.

It was the accident that brought her back. Only Ann knew that.

She grabbed her dad's hand and felt his calloused skin. She heard her mother's whisper, "Is that the eldest Kelly's girlfriend?"

Ann looked past the shoulders and heads of the people in front and saw Tony Kelly on the other side of the grave. Beside him was Patricia Hogan. She was in school uniform and had no make-up on. She wore her school jumper draped over her shoulders and the knot of her tie was at a rakish angle.

Ann closed her eyes. Tony Kelly had not contacted her, not so much as a telephone call.

"The blonde beside him," her mother continued.

Ann looked at her mother and felt a surge of hate. Rosie was lying in a box at the bottom of a hole and her mother was looking round to see who was who.

"I think so," she whispered and bent her head as if in prayer.

There was a congenial mumbling in the front room of the Kellys' house as people stood or sat with tiny glasses of whisky or sherry. Maureen O'Brien tried the sherry and shivered exaggeratedly.

"I suppose they've no gin" she said in a low voice. She was wearing a black skirt, a white blouse and a black cardigan. On her ear lobes there were two black stud earrings.

Ann had a glass of orange squash in her hand and was leaning against her dad.

Mr Kelly came towards them,

"I thank you for coming," he said. "It means a lot to Mrs Kelly." He had a glass of whisky in his hand and on his cheeks there were two red blotches as though someone had smudged a dollop of rouge there. He nodded his head to no one in particular and took a mouthful of drink.

For a few seconds nobody said anything. Finally John O'Brien said, "It's a dreadful business."

"It is. It is." Mr Kelly nodded his head again. Mrs Kelly was standing a few feet away with a plate of sandwiches in each hand. Her face was pale and looked pinched. She came towards them.

"Mrs O'Brien, have one," she said rather too loudly, "Red Salmon, a special offer. I have it a few weeks now." The plates were trembling slightly in her hands. Maureen O'Brien took a sandwich.

"It was a lovely service," she said. "The school-girls all there and in their uniforms. It's a tribute. You should be proud, Mrs Kelly."

Mrs Kelly continued as though she'd not heard, "My mother always said, whatever happens have a tin of ham or a tin of salmon in your cupboard. There's no disgrace then if someone comes unexpected. No disgrace."

Maureen O'Brien's face looked pained. "Mrs Kelly, if there's anything I can do . . ."

"The English have it with cucumber. We chop it up with a bit of onion and vinegar. I had a couple of tins actually. My mother always used to say, 'There's great comfort in a tin of salmon.'" The corners of Mrs Kelly's mouth turned upwards but the rest of her face was blank. Maureen O'Brien put her hand gently onto the other woman's arm but she was gone in a second, passing out more sandwiches to other mourners.

Maureen O'Brien put the uneaten sandwich down and drank the sherry in one mouthful.

"I'll just get another," she said and walked into the other room.

Ann looked round the room at the company

assembled there. There were quiet conversations and an occasional raised voice. No one was crying, not like in the church.

Her eyes rested on Tony and Patricia, who were standing together in the far corner of the room. For once, she and Patricia looked about the same age, both in their uniforms.

Had Patricia cried when Rosie got killed?

She stared at the older girl for a moment and tried to imagine what tears might do to all that composure and the make-up she usually wore. She tried to picture her red-faced, with black smudges under her eyes.

When Ann had first been Rosie's friend they'd laughed at Patricia and her make-up and her skinny legs. Rosie had said that one day the eyelashes wouldn't come off, that skin would grow over the bottoms of them and they would become part of Patricia's face. Later though, when they became friends, Patricia had given Rosie an old eye-shadow box with five colours and two brushes.

Rosie had spoken lightly of it but she'd been impressed. Patricia had won her over. It had been a cheap bribe, and Rosie had been taken in by it.

She looked away from the blonde girl and at Tony Kelly, who had his back to her.

He hadn't called her Annie, he hadn't even spoken to her. He'd avoided being near her and, if she accidentally came close to him, he'd averted his eyes.

It didn't matter.

Rosie was dead and nothing really mattered any more.

CHAPTER FIVE

The table was full of salmon sandwiches and fairy cakes and Ann's mother stood in her high heels and grey skirt and jumper looking at her watch.

"What time did you tell Rosemary?"

"It's Rosie, not Rosemary," Ann said with irritation. Her mother knew what Rosie's name was.

They stood looking at each other for a minute. All Ann had wanted was for Rosie to come over to her house to play some records and have a sandwich for tea.

She could have made the sandwich herself; her mum needn't have bothered to do anything. Why did she have to poke her nose in?

"Where's Dad?" she said. If Dad had been here, her mum wouldn't have been so bothered. On the other hand she might have been worse, introducing her dad like a prospective father-in-law.

"On the Isle of Dogs. Where else?"

"How come he's always working these days?"

Ann said, and immediately regretted it. She hadn't wanted to start her mother off.

"The house has to be paid for." Her mother said it in a sing-song voice as though it wasn't really her statement." If he did a bit less betting, though, maybe he wouldn't have to work all the hours . . . I don't see Dermot Duffy working all the hours."

Dermot Duffy was her dad's mate. He'd been a friend of the family ever since Ann could remember, but her mum still called him "Dermot Duffy" when she spoke of him as though he had to be singled out among all the Dermots that they might have known.

He was a steel erector like her dad, funny and nice, always giving Ann money for presents on her birthday and Christmas. He hadn't married, although her dad said he had had a fiancée in Dublin for twelve years.

"Where's my gerl then?" he'd say and Ann would sit on his lap and smell the faint odour of whisky on his breath.

"Here's a poem for you," he'd say and she'd sit braced with anticipation,

"There was an old lady from Spain,
Who cocked her leg over a train,
The train came past
And tickled her arse . . ."

Her mum always told him off for saying rude things to her and she would look at him behind her mother's back and see him mischievously winking.

Since they'd moved, she'd seen less of him, but occasionally she'd come home from school and find him sitting there sipping from a mug of tea and eating some crusty bread and butter.

She didn't run over and kiss or hug him like she had done when she was a little girl. She'd just say, "All right?"

And Dermot would answer, "Champion, gerl."

"Dermot's putting his money by, in a Deposit Account. He'll go back to Dublin with enough for a castle. You don't see his money thrown at the horses." Her mother was disgruntled. Now she would be even more touchy about Rosie when she came. In any case, it was untrue. Dermot was nearly always at the betting shop with her dad. It was just something for her mum to moan about.

"I've offered to go back to working in Jackson's, but no, he won't have that."

Ann watched as her mother folded her arms in resignation and glared at the triangular sandwiches and the pink and white iced cakes. Jackson's was the betting shop where she used to work.

"She must be a half hour late," her mother said.

"You go and watch the telly. I'll wait for Rosie . . ." Ann said.

The doorbell rang.

"Here she is." Ann felt a spurt of delight in her chest.

"About time too." Her mother followed her out into the hall.

* * *

"Your mum's nice," Rosie said, looking through the records.

"Um." Ann took a deep breath and handed her another cake. "You were a bit late."

It was the fifth fairy cake that Rosie had eaten. That plus at least four of the salmon sandwiches and some bread and butter.

"You got any Soul?" she said.

"No, I'm getting some for my birthday though." She was so pleased to have Rosie here. In Rosie's bag was a copy of *The Naked Jungle* that they were sharing. It was Ann's turn until the next day to read it. "And I might get a leather jacket."

"Patricia's got a blue leather," Rosie often used Tony's girlfriend as an arbiter of good taste when they were talking about clothes.

"And my mum's getting me some Levis."

"£150, Patricia's jacket cost!"

Ann frowned. She would never have a jacket that cost that.

"Dermot's promised me the money for some earrings. Nine carat!"

The two girls fell into silence.

Ann wanted to talk about all her things, her clothes and her new bedroom furniture that was promised at Christmas, but it was awkward. Rosie didn't have many things of her own. She shared a bedroom with a younger sister and some of her school clothes came from relatives. She rarely wore anything new or fashionable. She didn't even get regular pocket money. She just relied on her dad or her brother's generosity.

Glancing at the cover of her magazine, Ann saw, inside a yellow star, the words, "Win five hundred pounds' worth of clothes!"

"Look! What would you buy, if you won that?" She showed it to Rosie. It was a safe area; it was where they were equal, the world of make believe.

Rosie's face broke into a smile.

"Jeans, a leather jacket, boots, earrings . . ." Rosie's voice was like a train gathering speed out of a station.

"Hang on. Here's a bit of paper. Write it all down."

There was quiet as the two girls nibbled in concentration on the ends of two maroon school pencils. There was the whispering of mental arithmetic as they wrote down their lists.

"Oh!" It was Ann.

"What?"

"Mine comes to over five hundred pounds!"

"I've not finished mine yet."

The game was no good if you overspent. It was no good at all.

"Tell you what," Rosie said with sympathy. "Let's make it seven hundred and fifty."

Seven hundred and fifty pounds! It was simple! She looked at Rosie with admiration.

Rosie didn't have much, but with her anything was possible. She put a line through five hundred and wrote seven hundred and fifty.

When they went downstairs, her dad, Dermot and her mum were sitting in the front room.

"I'm just walking Rosie to the bus," she shouted.

"Let's have a look at your wee friend," Dermot shouted into the hall. Rosie screwed her face up.

"We haven't got time. Rosie's got to be home by seven."

Her dad's face appeared in the hall. It was covered in a thin powder of grey dust. There were two white circles round his eyes where his welding glasses had been.

"I'll run her home," he said, smiling at Rosie, "You can come as well. Bring her in to say hello to Dermot."

Dermot and her mother were sitting on the settee. Dermot had a light blue suit on and his face and hair shone from soap. His arm was stretched out along the back of the settee and at the very end of his fingers sat a cigarette.

"So this is your new friend, gerl." He smiled broadly. "What do you think, John? Do you think I could still get a girlfriend as good-looking as this one?" He laughed and the two girls looked away, embarrassed. Ann could smell his aftershave and noticed, for the first time a gold identity bracelet on his wrist.

Her dad laughed loudly and Ann looked at him. His clothes were filthy from work and his stomach stuck out between the end of his jumper and the beginning of his trousers. He looked in need of a good dust. He was rattling his car keys.

"Let's get going. Will I get you some wine, Maureen?"

"No. I've to watch my figure."

"Not at all . . ." They heard Dermot's voice as they followed her dad out of the room.

"We'll have some sweets, Dad." Ann said, linking her arm with Rosie's. Sweets to eat and *The Naked Jungle* to read. This was happiness.

She gave her dad's arm a quick squeeze as she went past. At the weekend she'd buy him some aftershave.

CHAPTER SIX

Just after Christmas they had their first real break-up.

Ann waited all weekend for a phone call from Rosie. On the Sunday night she sat in the front room by the door so that she could hear the phone if it rang. Her mother and father were watching a variety show on the television and she looked at the screen and thought about her row with Rosie.

They'd been due to go skating on the Saturday. Ann had been looking forward to it, she'd even chosen what she was going to wear. She'd told her mum and endured an inquisition about who was going, where they were meeting, what time she'd be back. She'd been told not to talk to strangers, not to get into anyone's car, not to smoke etc etc.

On Friday afternoon, just after the bell for the end of school, Ann said, "See you at the High Street about two."

"What?" Rosie had been packing her books away.

"About two. For skating."

"Oh. I can't go." Rosie said and continued packing. "My cousin and her family are coming round. They were away in Ireland at Christmas so we've still got to unwrap presents and stuff. Sorry, I forgot to say."

Ann looked at her in dismay. She visualised her jeans and boots and jumper laid out on the chair beside her bed ready for Saturday.

"You forgot?"

Rosie shrugged.

"That's great, that is." Ann's temper began to rise. "We made an arrangement and you forgot. Great!"

"Look, it's my cousin. She's my age. My mum likes me to be there."

"So you just forgot about an arrangement you made with me. Your family calls and you drop everything." Ann said "family" with bitterness. It wasn't fair.

"Come on," Rosie said. "We can go next week."

"If you can make it next week. If your 'family' don't have some other plans for you."

"I can't help it. I've got to be there. Give us a ring over the weekend."

"I doubt it. I doubt that I'll have time. I'll probably be doing something with my family." Ann had to raise her voice because Rosie was walking away from her towards the door of the classroom. One or two other girls had stopped talking and were looking at them.

"Please yourself," Rosie said and she was gone.

Ann watched the door of the classroom swing shut behind her.

"Do as you like," she said to no one in particular. "I'm sure I won't be ringing you over the weekend. I'll probably be busy."

She planned to spend Saturday morning doing her homework. She sat down at about nine thirty and wrote up notes on the First World War. She did some maths and some French verbs. Finally she read over a scene from Romeo and Juliet.

She was feeling hungry and went downstairs to see what was for lunch.

"It's only ten to eleven!" her mother said, and Ann looked at the clock in disbelief. It seemed as if she had been working for hours.

She read the paper and went over to the newsagent's for a couple of magazines. She clicked the telly on and off. She played her records.

At twelve she sat down and had a sandwich. The afternoon stretched ahead of her like a long empty road.

She walked out into the hall and looked angrily at the telephone as though it bore some responsibility for her having nothing to do. How often she had turned that dial to phone Rosie, to check if she'd done homework, to see if she'd watched a particular programme, just to speak to her.

How often had Rosie rung her?

She hadn't told her mother about the row. She'd said she'd changed her mind about going skating. Her mother had raised her eyebrows but said nothing. She knew about the row. Ann hadn't needed to say anything. She had read her dulled expression, her round shoulders, her silent sighs.

Her mum made pancakes and offered to hear the French verbs. She suggested a trip to the shops and hinted at the possibility of a treat of some sort. Ann knew it meant a new pair of tights or some item of make-up.

She said, "No, I don't fancy it," to all the offers.

She passed the phone several times in the afternoon and once or twice thought she would phone. It was silly, after all. Rosie had family commitments. Her mum had said she had to be there. It wasn't her fault, and Ann was blaming her for it.

But then she thought of Rosie sitting with her cousin, pulling the wrappers from late Christmas presents. She thought of them talking animatedly and then the phone would ring and someone would say, "It's for you Rosie. It's Ann."

Maybe Rosie would roll her eyes or sigh heavily, annoyed at being interrupted with her cousin. In her head, Ann could hear her friend saying, "I'll just get rid of her. Won't be a minute"

Underneath it all, Ann carried with her a niggling hurt that she had never been invited to Rosie's house. Rosie had been to tea at her house and dropped by a couple of times since, but she had never once asked Ann back.

Ann's throat began to feel sore, and she swallowed a couple of times. Her eyes glazed over and she thought she was going to cry. Giving the phone a contemptuous look, she went upstairs to her room and lay down on the bed.

On Sunday the phone rang two or three times in the morning. As soon as she heard the sharp ring her spirits lifted. It was going to be all right. Rosie would say sorry and maybe they could meet somewhere that afternoon. They'd laugh about the row and make plans to go skating the next Saturday. When the receiver was picked up and the ringing stopped, Ann's mood sank. It was Our Mary; it was Dermot Duffy for Dad; it was Lil from the flats.

After lunch, Ann went to her room and sat down in front of her mirror and decided to make plans. She would be friends with Rosie if Rosie rang her before she went to bed that evening. Otherwise she would not. She would go to the library on the way home from school on Monday and find out the addresses of youth clubs. She was far too dependent on Rosie anyway.

She glanced at her reflection and saw that she was smiling. She combed her fingers through her hair and shook her head a couple of times. Wetting her forefinger, she smoothed her eyebrows and took a critical look at her features. Not bad, not bad at all, she thought.

During tea she felt in high spirits. She was not going to ring Rosie. There was certainty in her head about this. She had been in the right and Rosie was the one who had to apologize. She ate her tea with vigour, she ironed her school clothes, she packed her bag.

After the variety show was over, she felt desolate. She looked out into the hall and saw the edge of the table that held the phone. After all she'd said to herself, after all the plans she'd made, the only thing she wanted to do was to go out and phone Rosie. She kept swallowing back the lump of frustration that she felt in her throat and going over in her head the rights and wrongs of it.

Rosie hadn't thought about it at all. She'd been busy all weekend with her family and her cousin of the same age.

And Ann hadn't even been invited to Rosie's house.

Just before ten she got up, and closing the front room door behind her, went out into the hall and began to dial Rosie's number.

CHAPTER SEVEN

Rosie's house was a riot of noise, activity and disarray. Ann had never seen such a messy place. In every room there were small cars and dolls littering the floor, and each corner was hidden with mounds of clothes, clean or dirty, Ann didn't know. Ann counted three children under the age of five, one of whom was in a big black pram in the hall. Every time Mrs Kelly passed she gave it a substantial nose wipe and tucked a blanket over its feet. There were one or two older Kellys loitering around on the pavement outside.

There were coats which had mounted the banister eight or nine deep, and when Ann gave her coat to Mrs Kelly she noticed her trying to fit it on top of them. After a few seconds, realizing it wouldn't go, Mrs Kelly lifted three or four of the coats off into her arms and placed Ann's on the banister instead.

She was still holding the coats while making a cup of tea in the kitchen. Ann felt she ought to take them off her but wasn't sure where she should put them.

Mrs Kelly always seemed to be holding things as though her arms were some kind of pending tray, waiting to find a corner or shelf or drawer on which things could go.

Rosie was changing upstairs and Ann and Mrs Kelly were standing awkwardly in the kitchen waiting for the kettle to boil. Tony Kelly came in and said, "Hello there, Annie." She had never been called "Annie" before, not even by Dermot Duffy. She had always made a big deal out of the way people spelled her name "Ann without an E" she'd say, insisting that it gave the word a different sound. She smiled with pleasure at the familiarity.

He was looking for something to polish his shoes with.

"Here," Mrs Kelly said, giving him the first thing to hand.

Ann watched him as he rubbed each side of the shoe with a blue and red tea towel, making small circles on the leather. After a couple of minutes he stood back from them and smiled. "See your face in them, Annie?" he said, and laughed, flinging the tea towel to the side where it joined a variety of other things that had met with the floor.

"Are you seeing that Patricia woman?" Mrs Kelly said, putting two of the coats on the side by the fridge.

"Yes." He said it with a sigh, as though he expected some trouble.

"Make sure you get her home on time. I don't want her da ringing here again."

"Yes, yes."

"And make sure you don't take her into a bar. Remember what Father Patrick said."

"Yes, yes, yes. Anything else? Shall I make sure I don't enjoy myself!" He said it good-naturedly, rolling his eyes at Ann. Ann picked up two used cornflakes dishes and held them while Mrs Kelly put the other two coats across the table. For a moment her hands were free and she looked lost as though she were trying to remember what to do with them. She bent over and opened the oven door and took out a tray of tarts.

"Shall I wash a few things up?" Ann said after Tony had gone. The sink was full of plates and bowls and mugs and Mrs Kelly was arranging the jam tarts onto a two-tier cake stand.

"Would you, love? There's a girl. I wouldn't mind," she continued," but her da and ma come from Dublin. They think they're somebody. He's always on the phone, his daughter this, his daughter that."

Rosie came into the kitchen, followed by her father.

"This is Ann, is it?" her father said, and smiled. He reached across and picked up one of the jam tarts. "And what do you think of Mrs Kelly's cooking, Ann?"

"Very nice," Ann said. She placed the tea towel on top of a pile of dishes and picked up a jam tart.

Later, on the way to the bus stop, Rosie said, "I've got another book here." She patted her shoulder bag.

"Does Tony know we read his books?"

"Yes. But he won't say nothing."

"He's still going out with Patricia, then." Ann said it with a sigh.

"Nearly a year now. He's bought her a swivel thing on a chain and when you spin it, it says, 'I love you'."

Ann visualized the chain and Tony holding each end of it ready to put it on someone's neck.

"Which book?" she said, without thinking.

"*After The Love Has Gone*. By that man who wrote *Movietown Nights*."

"Great. That was a great book."

"We can go down the park and start reading it together."

Ann threaded her arm through Rosie's and they quickened their pace.

Sitting on the bench near the lake an hour or so later, Ann said,

"Do you think people really do those sorts of things. In real life?"

She said "In real life" in a dismal way. It was a phrase that had always meant the bursting of bubbles, the shattering of dreams. There was no Father Christmas "in real life"; there was no possibility of her ever meeting any of her favourite pop stars "in real life"; there was no chance of her becoming a film star "in real life".

"They must do. It doesn't sound made up." Rosie said, looking up from the page.

"But . . . why don't they get pregnant . . . or caught?"

"It don't matter if they do. They're rich."

That was it. The books were full of good looking, rich people who seemed to live on an entirely different sort of planet to the one she knew. They drove aeroplanes, speedboats, fast cars; the men had beautiful wives or mistresses. They climbed up mountains and skied down them, sometimes stopping on the way to make love. They played endless games of roulette and changed their clothes three or four times a day, and every time someone came to see them they opened a bottle of champagne.

They didn't have bills to pay or jobs to go to. They didn't have to get planning permission to take a wall down or get someone to look after small kids when they were going out.

Ann thought of her dad, caked with dirt after a day on site. She thought of Rosie's mum, up to her knees in children, jam tarts in the oven.

Her parents just met each other in Belfast and got married. She'd heard her mum say something like that the other day, in the middle of a row with her dad.

"I met you. We went out together. We got married." She'd spat it out, leaving long gaps between each of the sentences. Anne remembered how she'd looked when she said it, her arms folded across her chest and one leg folded around the other like a physical plait.

Ann looked across the park. "God!" She said in desperation.

"Yes?" It was a joke Rosie always made.

"I'm so fed up. Why doesn't anything exciting ever happen to us?"

Rosie closed the book.

"We could make it happen."

"What?"

"Don't know. Meet some boys maybe."

"Where?"

"Outside the college. Maybe see some of Tony's friends."

St John's College was at Wood Green. It was too far to go to straight after school. All the boys would have gone home by then.

"How will we get there in time?"

"We'll bunk off one afternoon."

"Bunk off?" Ann's mother's face leapt into her head. "I couldn't. I'd get killed."

"Huh! Now you know why nothing exciting ever happens. You've got to take chances for things to happen. You're nearly fifteen, aren't you?"

"Where would we go all afternoon, before the boys came out of school?"

"We could go to the Wimpy; up round the park; over to Ally Pally. Anywhere!"

"What about a note?"

"We wouldn't need a note. We'd go to afternoon registration and then on the way to whatever lesson it is we could slip out the side door. If we're missed we can say that one of us felt ill and went out to the chemist to get some aspirins. No, even better. We'll say one of us came on and we had to get some sanitary towels. Nobody would ever question that! We'll say we didn't think the nurse

71

would have anything like that. We can say we were too embarassed to tell anyone. We'd get a telling off but they wouldn't think we'd been bunking."

"But how would we know if we had been missed or not?"

"They'd ring home."

Ann saw her mother holding the phone and a look of fury appear on her face.

"I couldn't. At least, I have to think about it. Do it on an afternoon when my mum's going out." She looked at Rosie, pleased with herself for having made a decision.

"Don't take too long," Rosie said, going back to the book. "You've only got one lifetime."

CHAPTER EIGHT

On the morning of the day they'd decided to bunk, Ann was looking at the newspaper on the kitchen table while her mother was buttering toast by the grill. The radio was on and Ann absentmindedly tapped her fingers on the table. She should never have agreed to bunk off school.

She picked up the toast and took a half-hearted nibble.

The front door slammed hard and made them both jump. Her dad had left for work.

"Was that John?" her mother said aloud. Ann ignored the remark.

"It bloody was!" Her mother walked across and peered out of the front window. "Would you credit that? Without a word, he's off!"

It was like her dad. So often he seemed totally preoccupied. He might be all over her one minute and the next look through her as though she were a stranger. Or she might be explaining some long piece of history or something she'd learnt in school and he'd be agreeing or asking questions. Then her mum would come in or the news would come on the telly and he'd be irked by what she was saying, terse in his answers, his gaze being drawn away.

"It's just like him." Her mother said it in an angry voice.

Ann continued to look at the paper, a piece of uneaten toast perched in her hand. She had packed her jeans and top and put her pocket money in the zip pocket of her bag.

There was a huge ball of guilt in her stomach as though she'd already done the deed; as though it were the morning after bunking off, not the morning before.

It amazed her that feelings could transform themselves into physical sensations. Even though she had had nothing for breakfast her stomach felt full up to the top of her throat, as though someone had put a straw in her mouth and blown her full of air. Just looking at the piece of toast made her feel mildly nauseous.

Her absence from school would be noticed. Her mother would be rung up and told. Even if that didn't happen they would be seen somewhere, at Turnpike Lane or Ally Pally. Rosie had said they would act like French students if they were approached. If a policeman came up to them they would say, "Je ne comprend pas," and then say, "Nous allons à Alexandra Palace," all of which Rosie had worked out using her French vocabulary book.

But in the middle of all that play-acting, one

of her mum's friends would be walking past and come over to see what she was doing, talking to a policeman in a part of London where she shouldn't be, at a time of day when she should be in school.. Either that or her dad would be driving around and look out of his truck window and there she would be.

It was all too awful to think about. She put the toast back down on the plate. She would just continue to look at the paper for another ten minutes and then she could go. Then it would be too late for her mother to notice the bulk of her school bag or perhaps to suggest suddenly that she would drop by school at the end of the afternoon to meet her.

"Just like you to ignore it." Her mother said suddenly with a tone of nastiness in her voice. "You're just the same as him. It's just the sort of thing you'd do, go out without saying goodbye. My mother always said, it might be the last time you ever see that person alive. The last time ever. They might go out and be hit by a car, run into the very ground and you'd never have said goodbye."

Ann looked at her mother, resplendent in a red and white check dress, her hair hanging in corkscrew curls, red button earrings that looked like Smarties and would no doubt match whatever colour lipstick she was going to put on. In the normal course of events she'd have bitten back, made some provoking comment. It would only be fair. Her father had been inconsiderate and wasn't there to be rowed with and she got the blame.

She said nothing. Instead she put her breakfast things on the worktop. She kept quiet while she put her blazer on. Her mother had put rubber gloves on and was circling a spot on the cooker with an Ajax pad.

As she went out of the kitchen door she turned. "Goodbye, Mother", she said, enunciating the words.

Walking down the path, she thought, I've nothing to feel guilty about. Who can blame me for doing what I'm doing after being treated like that?

Once they'd changed into their jeans and tops, Rosie had a brainwave.

"It's Wednesday!" she said.

"Yes?" Ann was looking up and down Wood Green High Road, squinting her eyes into the faces of passers-by. There might be one that she knew. Millions of people shopped there.

"That's the day me mum goes to Kathleen's."

"Yes?" Ann's eyes followed a panda car as it drove slowly past. What if a policeman stopped and spoke to them in fluent French? She wished she had paid more attention in French lessons. She resolved to learn ten words a day. In a year's time she'd know three and a half thousand French words . . .

Rosie was looking at her. She'd said something she hadn't heard.

"Sorry?"

"Me mum's out at me Auntie Kathleen's. The house's empty. We can go back there for an hour or so before we go to St John's."

"What about the kids?"

"She takes Patsy and Brendan. The rest are at school. They go there straight from school, anyroad. So there'll be no one there until about five."

"Are you sure?" Ann said it uneasily. She was sure there were more Kellys than that. In her mind she had images of them peeping out of every corner of that house; from behind queues of coats, under layers of ironing, in among huge pile ups of miniature cars or in the middle of an extended family of dolls.

"There won't be anyone there!" Rosie started to walk off up the road.

"What about your neighbours?" Ann shouted as she quickened her step to keep up with her.

At first, when they got there, the house seemed empty. It was quiet and peaceful, much more so than her own house when she went into it. It had the feel of a church about it and for the first time Ann noticed the statues of Our Lady and the Sacred Heart and the little vial of holy water by the front door. It was the contrast that made it seem so quiet. Her house was never noisy. Rosie's house had been full of noise and activity the couple of times that she had been there. Now it was not.

They went into the kitchen and Rosie went straight over to the fridge and opened the door. It was something she always did whenever her mother wasn't there. She stood for a few moments just perusing the contents. Ann found it difficult to understand. Food was of no interest to her at all. Her mother was always trying to get her to eat different delicacies. The previous week she had put a cooked pineapple ring on top of a piece of bacon and Ann had screwed her nose up exaggeratedly until, amidst a volley of "tuts", it had been removed.

Rosie took two slices of bread from a packet on the cupboard.

"Want some?" she said.

"No."

It was then that they heard what sounded like the front door slamming.

"Who's that?" Ann whispered unnecessarily.

"Ssh!" Rosie took a bite from the dry bread. She walked towards the door, "I was feeling sick so you came home with me, right? You changed on the way and I've just changed upstairs, right? She'll never check. She'll never ring your mum."

Ann stood rigid, her stomach ballooning up with fright, watching Rosie bite into her piece of bread again. She probably wouldn't get into much trouble. Perhaps her parents wouldn't mind so much. She saw her own mother's face that morning, her thin pale lips and the straight lines that sat across her forehead.

The kitchen door opened and Tony Kelly came in. He was dressed in Jeans and nothing else. His bare feet stuck out from beneath his jeans, and round his neck was a thin gold chain. He looked flustered and jumped slightly when he saw them.

"What are you doing here?" he said, his voice

sounding unbearably loud against their previous whispers.

"What are you doing here? And who was that?" Rosie pushed past him and ran up the hall and Ann could hear the front door opening.

"You've bunked off," he said, smiling, relaxing. Ann smiled back at him, embarrassed, not knowing what to say.

Rosie came back into the room. "What was she doing here? How come she wasn't at school?"

"Never you mind. What will Mum say when I tell her her beloved Rose is bunking from the convent?"

"Nothing to what she'll say when she finds out that you and Patricia have been here while she's round at Kathleen's."

They both looked at each other and Tony held a mock fist up at Rosie.

"And how will she find that out?"

"I wouldn't tell her. Not if you made it worth my while." Rosie was smiling. It was all jokes now, all a game.

"If you don't tell her about me and Patricia, I won't tell her about you and wee Annie," he said, using an Irish accent for "wee Annie" as though he were copying his mother.

"At least make us a cup of tea." Rosie was tearing at her bread with her teeth, as though she hadn't eaten for days.

"I was just going to. Just about to put the kettle on for my sister and her 'wee chum'." He got up and, taking Ann in his arms as though he were about to do some ballroom dancing, he whirled her round away from the place where the kettle and teapot were and sat her down at the table.

"One sugar or two?" He said laying a grubby-looking tea towel over his arm and bending slightly as though he were a waiter in a posh restaurant.

Going up to the toilet later, Ann had to pass Tony's room. She'd been in it once before when Rosie had shown her all his books. She'd thought at the time how it had been a total contrast to the rest of the house, everything in its place, the bed neatly made, books and magazines stacked tidily on shelves.

The door was open and she ignored it on her way to the toilet. On her way back she couldn't stop herself from peeping in.

On a bedside chair Tony's trousers were laid neatly, the creases folded together. His shirt was around the back of the chair and hanging down the middle was his striped tie. Underneath were his shoes, a sock tucked in each one. On a hanger, hooked onto the wardrobe door, was his brown blazer with the yellow piping.

The light on the record player was on and a black disc sat silently on the deck.

The bed was unmade, at least it looked as though it had been slept in, the covers pulled diagonally across, the pillows at funny angles.

It gave her a strange stab of excitement to look at it. It was the sort of feeling she occasionally got when she was reading one of Tony's books. She turned and went down the stairs.

By three fifteen they were shivering down the road from St John's. The boys were due out at about half past, although a number of the sixth-formers had been drifting out for some time.

"They get free time, Tony says, because of the A levels."

"Oh." It seemed a good idea to Ann. Just go into school when you wanted to, or if you had special classes that led to special exams.

"What's Tony doing?"

"English, French and History."

Ann shook her head in disbelief. It was one thing having to do all those things but to choose to go back to school and do poems and speak French and learn dates was too much.

"He does like reading." She said it as though she knew him very well. The cold seemed to penetrate her top and she shivered. She'd lost interest in looking at the boys coming out of St John's. In her mind she kept picturing Tony Kelly's room. His clothes folded over the chair, the bed unmade. She hadn't seen Patricia, but Rosie had seen her disappearing out of the gate.

"You could put your blazer on if you like."

"No, I'm all right," she lied.

"Here they come!" Rosie said. In the distance groups of boys sloped round the corners of the gate, some chattering, some pushing and gesticulating, one or two running ahead of the others. They were mostly the young ones, for whom the school bell was like a starting pistol.

It was then that Ann noticed the blue Ford pulling in across the road. No longer interested in who was coming out of the school, she gazed across the four lanes of traffic at it. It looked familiar and all at once she remembered that she was somewhere she wasn't supposed to be. As Rosie moved out to the edge of the kerb to get a better look at the boys, she stepped in behind her, close to an overgrown hedge.

A man got out of the driver's side and at first it was only the suit that she recognized. It was light blue and had a faint shine.

It was Dermot Duffy, not at work, not even in his work clothes.

"My God!" she said,

"Yes?" Rosie smiled at her, but seeing her face, turned and looked across the road.

"It's my dad's mate," said Ann. She was sure then that her dad would get out of the other side. The job had probably finished early. Dermot and her dad had gone home and changed and gone back out for a drink and a bet. Why they should be at Wood Green she couldn't fathom.

Rosie walked towards her and they both stepped into the pathway of the house and pushed themselves into the side of the hedge.

"I knew it! I knew someone would see us. I knew it!"

"Ssh! He hasn't seen us. We'll wait until they go in somewhere and then we'll shoot off. They'll never know. Lucky you seen them first." Rosie was as calm as ever.

What if it was your dad, she wanted to say. What if your dad had just walked along, what then? But she couldn't speak. It was as though he had already seen her and she was bracing herself for the row and the repercussions. She felt her eyes glazing over, even though she hadn't thought she was going to cry.

But something stopped the tears.

They dried up as she looked across the road, through the gap between the two buses, and saw Dermot Duffy's passenger door open. The cold spring breeze caught the corners of a coat and blew them apart to reveal a red and white check dress. A young attractive woman stood on the pavement her face beaming with a smile, red button earrings and red lipstick.

Maureen O'Brien, her hair blowing here and there, laughing gaily at something as she slammed the car door.

Her mother with Dermot Duffy; her dad was nowhere around.

PART THREE

Questions

Ann O'Brien sat on a bench in the cemetery. The heat from the sun was heavy on her shoulders and she watched as two wasps circled round and round a piece of uneaten orange that had been dropped on the ground.

There was no headstone on Rosie's grave yet, just a small wooden cross with her name on. The wreaths had all been removed, but there were three or four potted plants and a small terracotta vase that held a bunch of chrysanthemums.

It was the day before she was due to go back to school and she was playing a game in her head that she sometimes used to play when she was on her own and had nothing to do.

What was I doing This Time Last Year? she thought.

It had been the day before starting her new school. She'd been living in the new house for a couple of months. She'd bought her uniform and was ready for the fourth year. She'd tried to imagine what it would be like being the new girl, trying to make new friends. She'd wondered about the teachers and the lessons and the dinners.

Was it then that her mum and dad had started rowing about money and her dad had begun to work weekends and late nights? Certainly her mum had begun to feel lonely and miss the hustle and bustle of living in the flats; and then there was her job that she'd had to give up because her dad hadn't liked it. Ann remembered her wandering aimlessly from room to room in the new house while Ann had been making plans, thinking about the future . . .

It was a time when Dermot Duffy was always in and out.

It was the time before she knew Rosie.

It was months before she had met Tony Kelly.

This Time Last Year, she thought, Tony Kelly and Rose Kelly didn't exist.

For a moment Ann O'Brien held her lips tightly together and looked away from Rose Kelly's grave. She took shallow breaths and held her eyelids open in case she blinked out the tears that were forming there.

Oh Rosie, she thought, how different things were then. She smiled, thinking of herself in a new house, with a new uniform hanging in the wardrobe, a new pencil case and school bag sitting in the hall by the front door.

It was something she found herself doing increasingly, addressing Rosie in her head, as though there was another world in there where Rosie moved around and lived, where nothing bad had happened, where they were still friends.

Sometimes she allowed herself to get into moods where she imagined Rosie hadn't been killed at all. She let herself think that Rosie had been sent to Ireland the way that Fran had been. Rosie's parents had found out that Ann and their daughter had been reading dirty books and drinking alcohol. They'd sent their daughter to a Catholic convent in a remote part of Waterford. Rosie was to stay there until she had done her A levels.

Ann kept her eyes off Rosie's grave and made herself look between two of the trees in the distance where she couldn't see any stones or statues, just bushes and sky and some cars passing outside the railings. She imagined it was a view she could see from the window of a pale room in which there was an old-fashioned desk with a swivel chair. There was blue notepaper and envelopes on the top of the desk and she could see herself straightening her skirt so that it didn't get wrinkled when she sat down on it. She had a thoughtful expression on her face and she saw herself writing in a uniform script a letter to Rosie.

Dear Rosie, (she would write)
How are you? How's the strict convent life? I heard a joke the other day which I thought I'd tell you. What sex life do priests have? They have nun. Get it? "Nun"! (Rosie would laugh at that.)
I've had a hell of a summer. My mum and

dad have been knocking walls down and I've been carting out plastic buckets of rubbish to my dad's work truck. At least he's not working so much now as he used to. My mum wears a scarf round her hair and old trousers and a shirt but she still puts her make-up on and amid all the dust and smoke she smells of scent and talcum powder.

My dad spends his time measuring and cutting bits of wood and drawing diagrams on the wall of how it will all look when it's finished. Then he sweeps it all up into little piles which me and my mum pick up with some spare bits of hardboard.

My mum seems happier now, but I still worry about her. If she goes up the shops I count the time it takes her. If she goes out on her own in the evening I watch the clock till she comes back.

She and my dad don't seem to row as much now, and the other day I heard them actually talking about her getting another part-time job. My mum was showing him the newspaper ads and my dad was sitting, listening, without getting the hump.

I haven't seen Dermot Duffy for weeks. My mum says he's in Ireland – although I haven't asked.

You won't believe this, but I go to the library nearly every day. The woman in there knows me. I'm reading detective stories by American writers. Every time I go up to the counter she *says, "You're fast. You must be reading every other page," and I smile and say, "No, just every other line." Every day she says it and every day I give the same answer.*

What are you . . . (she wanted to write "reading" but couldn't continue the sentence).

The game only went so far. Asking questions that needed answers stretched credibility. Even she couldn't extend her imagination to the point where the postman placed a white envelope in her hand that had a Waterford post mark on it.

She saw herself sitting in the pale room, staring out of the window into the trees and the sky. It was the very things she couldn't include in her letter that she needed to say the most.

The writer took a deep breath and leant forward with her pen.

Somebody got killed a few months ago (she saw herself writing). *A girl of my age got run over by a lorry. It was about three thirty in the afternoon and it was a sweaty day. The girl didn't see the lorry, didn't know it was there. It just rose up out of the tarmac and came thundering towards her. They say she flew into the air and hit the ground just to the side of the lorry's path. They say it was a blessing for her parents that she didn't go under, that her body wasn't squashed by the big wheels. They say she just thoughtlessly ran out. They don't know, though. They don't know that it was my fault.*

What do you think of that? One minute, this girl had a bus to catch, homework to do, tea to eat. The next, there was just blackness. It must have been like someone flicking a light switch off.

And it was my fault.

In the cemetery Ann O'Brien unfolded a tissue from a wad in her pocket. She blew her nose and wiped her eyes and the sides of her mouth. This Time Last Year her biggest problem was where she would sit in class and whether she would get a matching wardrobe and dressing table for her new bedroom. She shook her head.

Somewhere in her chest there was a ball of anger. She got up and looked at the one remaining wasp that was clinging to the piece of orange.

She lifted her foot and viciously squashed the wasp into the ground. Without looking back, she folded her arms and walked slowly up the path.

Kate Martin used the stapler gun fiercely against the wall. She was furious. Taking another piece of work from the pile, she placed it at angles from the rest and aimed the gun. Kate hated symmetry. She liked things to be odd-looking, eye-catching.

On the table beside her was her copy of *Modern Women Poets*. Just looking at it made her anger boil again.

"It's unsuitable, I'm afraid," Sister Dominic had

said. "Our parents wouldn't like their daughters to read this kind of thing at all. Oh no, not at all."

Kate had tried to argue. How good the writers were, how the poems were relevant to modern day living, how they could be a focus for moral questions.

Sister Dominic had smiled. "That may well be," she'd said, "but these are young girls. Are we really to trouble them with the knowledge of adultery, abortion," she'd looked up and down the corridor before lowering her voice to a conspiratorial whisper, "and pre-marital intercourse?"

Kate had wanted to laugh out loud.

"Let's stick to John Keats," she'd said. "He's done very well for us so far." And she'd walked off, her rosary beads clattering together all the way down the corridor.

Kate sat down in her classroom after she'd finished sticking up the wall display. Ann O'Brien was due to come and see her soon.

Was she really so wrong to want the girls to learn a bit about real life? Only a few months ago another sixth-former had had to leave because she was pregnant. No one had known, Kate had only found out because she'd seen her in Enfield Town shopping with her mother, her stomach camouflaged behind a loose-fitting coat.

Kate felt listless and angry. For five years she'd taught English in this school, she'd been friends with all the staff, had been to tea at the convent and mixed with many of the parents.

She had professional judgement. She knew what was good for the girls.

She let the staple gun rest on the desk and leaned back in her chair.

What does it matter? she suddenly thought. What does any of it matter? A picture of Rose Kelly's body lying on the road flashed into her head. In the corner of the picture stood Ann O'Brien holding one of her dead friend's shoes, her face shocked, looking for a brief moment as though she was going to laugh. It was like an old photograph, and for some reason Kate kept looking at it over and over again.

Kate hadn't cried over Rose Kelly's death as some of the other staff had done, but she had felt differently about things since. Many of the other teachers had children of their own and Kate had watched tears forming in their eyes whenever the accident was discussed. (You'd not know, they'd said to her, not being married, not having any children yourself.) Kate had felt shocked and saddened and had wanted to cry just to spite them all, but whenever she thought of the lorry and the dead girl she felt frustration and not tears forming inside her. For everyone else it was all over. The girl had stupidly run into the road and been killed. But Kate couldn't understand it. There had been no reason to run into the road. There was no bus stop opposite, there were no sweet shops across the road and Rosie had left her schoolbag down on the pavement that she was crossing away from.

Nobody else thought it was a mystery. Kate was

the only one. Everyone told her not to worry about it, that teenagers did stupid things, that there was too much traffic on the road anyway, that it was a wonder more people weren't killed every single day.

Kate found herself feeling irritated by everyday things that didn't normally annoy her; the way that other teachers in the staff room guarded their lockers; the fact that they had their own personal supplies of milk and sugar in small well-washed-out jam-jars; Sister Dominic's unannounced entrances into her classroom when she was in the middle of something; these things were totally unconnected with the accident but for some reason, when she was irked by them, she came back to thinking about Rose Kelly and a moment or so later the photograph would form in her head.

The girl was dead and it wasn't the fault of the staff or Sister Dominic – or the Church, come to that – but she felt peeved at all of them.

There was a quiet knock on the door and Kate said, "Come in. The door's not locked."

She sat Ann O'Brien down in a chair by the window next to her desk, which was covered in files and registers. Ann looked and then immediately looked away towards the window.

"How are you, Ann?"

"Fine," she answered and then there was silence. The noise of the girls playing in the playground sounded as though it were streets away instead of just a few feet below on the other side of the window.

"I thought we'd just have a little talk," Kate

said, but was faced with an unflinching gaze. Ann shrugged her shoulders and looked over towards the wall display.

Ann O'Brien wasn't fine and Kate Martin knew it. She had been back at school a week now and there had been the six weeks' holiday since the funeral.

She'd mostly been on her own, even though Kate had seen sympathetic girls trying to make friends, offering to sit next to her. She'd been silent in class, working mostly by herself, unaided, without being nagged.

It was nine or so weeks since the accident, and Kate had expected Ann to come back to school and be full of emotion about the loss of her friend. She had expected Ann to be pained by the very business of coming back to school and the memories that might be attached to the place of her and Rose Kelly.

But Ann O'Brien was tight lipped and seemed controlled at all times. Kate looked at her as she gazed out of the classroom window. She looked bored. It was the kind of expression that a lot of teenagers adopted just before they were due to be told off, as though they were anticipating every word that was about to be said to them, as though they knew it all.

"I thought you might like to talk to me about Rose. I imagine it's quite painful coming back to school."

Ann shrugged her shoulders and said nothing. Kate was stumped for words.

They sat in silence and Kate wondered what to

do next. She had wanted to talk to Ann for a couple of reasons. She was genuinely concerned about the girl and the experience she had been through. She was also the key to why Rose stepped out into the road. She'd been hazy about it at the coroner's hearing, pleading that she "couldn't explain" or "didn't remember" but Kate couldn't accept these statements. The whole business must have been the biggest thing in this young girl's life. It wasn't that she couldn't remember but that she didn't want to remember.

Kate remembered her strange expression in church almost as though she was bracing herself for some blow.

It had been as though she feared something.

The whole thing was a puzzle, but in the end Kate would have let it drop. She would have just shrugged her shoulders and got on with things had she not stumbled on something odd about the day that Rose Kelly had been killed.

Part of her job was to check the form registers against the subject registers. She did it randomly every four weeks or so, catching odd episodes of truancy and checking up on lateness.

At the beginning of the new school year Kate took Rose Kelly's class register and checked back over the last week of the summer term. She looked into the register and noted a line of discreet O's indicating that Rose was absent. It seemed more sensitive than drawing a line through her name. She looked at the subject registers and saw, to her satisfaction, that the teachers had all done the same thing. She couldn't resist turning the pages and going back to the day of the accident. For some reason she wanted to see the "present" mark against Rose Kelly's name on the last day, on the last lesson that she ever attended.

The regular teacher had been absent and a supply teacher had filled in the red marks in the column. Kate looked at it for a moment and felt sadness welling up inside her. The class had had Art for the whole afternoon. It had been Rose's last ever Art lesson. Had she started a drawing? Had there been a half-done sketch of hers in the cupboard that they had put in a parcel to be sent to Mrs Kelly at some later date?

It was then that she noticed the black nought a few names down. It was beside Ann O'Brien's name. According to the register, Ann O'Brien had not been present on the afternoon of Rose Kelly's death. Kate frowned. Ann had been at the accident. She had been in school uniform. She had not said she had been absent.

Kate looked at the class register. Ann had been marked "present" by her form teacher. Had the supply teacher made a mistake? Had she, not knowing Ann, simply not heard her answer when she marked the register?

Or had Ann been absent? Had she truanted and for some reason come back to school at the end of the afternoon?

Why hadn't anyone noticed?

Her class had been taken by a supply teacher, a woman they didn't normally use who had done a couple of days and then moved on to another school. She was bound to have heard of the accident, but perhaps she hadn't put two and two together. How could she?

Kate and the other teachers knew the girls well. They knew who was friends with who. They would have picked up the absence.

Why wasn't it picked up the following week when the regular teacher returned?

Kate had thought hard about this.

Because no one had been thinking about Ann O'Brien. Everyone had been concentrating on Rose Kelly.

"Ann, I've noticed something odd in the registers." Ann O'Brien turned away from the window and looked at Kate. "It seems that you were absent on the afternoon that Rose was killed. Can you explain that?" Ann lowered her eyes and looked at her hands. Her expression seemed to relax for a moment and Kate realized that the previous hard look on her face had been a mask.

"Is there something you would like to tell me?"

Ann O'Brien started to shake her head slowly.

"Why were you not in school? What were you doing outside school in your uniform if you were truanting? It doesn't make sense."

There was a long gap during which the sound of an ice cream van playing *Popeye the Sailor Man* intruded into the room. Suddenly it stopped and there was quiet.

"Does it have something to do with Rose?" she said gently.

"No, no," Ann said, and she put the back of her hand up to her mouth.

"Where were you?" Kate pushed.

"I don't know!" Ann's voice was breaking and Kate saw that she was biting hard into her hand. She was starting to cry, so Kate opened her drawer and got a box of tissues out. She felt in control again. Tears were something she could deal with.

Ann mumbled something into the tissue.

"What?" Kate said.

She spoke again but her words were covered with sniffs and coughs.

Kate waited until she had quietened. She held a bunch of tissues in mid-air towards her. Ann O'Brien looked straight at her.

"I did it," she said. "I pushed her onto the road. I pushed Rosie under the lorry."

Too shocked to say anything, Kate watched as the girl seemed to fold up in front of her; her shoulders rounded, her elbows sunk into her diaphragm, her head bowed. For a moment, Kate felt as though she was stuck to the chair, watching the girl trembling as though it was snow and sleet hitting the window and not lazy rays of autumnal sunshine.

Pulling herself together, she got up and walked round the desk and put her arms round the sobbing girl.

CHAPTER NINE

Ann watched her mother get ready for the dance at the Excelsior. She supposed, in an old-fashioned sort of way, her mother was attractive. She dressed a bit oddly, though; she had all sorts of little things like earrings and beads and stuff on her shoes that matched whatever it was that she was wearing.

Her dad was still sleeping in front of the telly.

She looked at her mother's dress. It had vivid pinks and deep blues all swirling around in a pattern. It was revolting, but she wouldn't say it. It was tight at the waist and the skirt fell in layers. It was also quite low at the front and the line between her breasts looked as though it had been drawn with a felt tip.

Thank God her mother had stopped dressmaking for her.

Ann thought back to the years of having stiff, nylon dresses and small pouch bags that matched, making her look like someone off an old Christmas card. At one time, when she was about eight, her mother had become so proficient at sewing that she made her virtually every piece of clothing that she could want, coats, trousers, skirts, tops, nighties, dresses; it was only her knickers, vests and socks that she still bought from Marks & Spencer's.

One of her mother's favourite ploys was to make herself a dress and then, from the same fabric, make Ann one too.

The three of them might go out to a wedding or to a "do" at The Irish Centre and her father would beam with pride at his two women, one clever and attractive (beautiful she had heard him call her) and the other a skinny kid in a stiff dress.

She couldn't quite remember when she had stopped being proud of these outfits with lace that stood bolt upright and bits of red or blue velvet sewn into the sleeves and neck. It had been about the same time that she had refused any more home perms.

It was when she'd had to wear a school uniform that her mother had lessened her hold. It was then that she'd started to grow her hair long and straight. It had looked untidy, but it was better than the halo of frizz that came from the bits of tissue paper and the perm curlers. Enough was enough.

I'm not a doll that you can play with, comb my hair, dress me up, change my looks, paint my face, she'd wanted to say to her mother, like they did in the films. But she'd said nothing, because off screen people didn't tell each other The Truth like that.

She'd tucked wayward strands of her hair behind her ears and refused offers of home-made dresses, skirts or anything else.

She was wearing a black skirt, her knee-length boots and a green jumper. Her mother looked at her in distaste.

"Are you sure you won't let me do your hair? I've the curling brush here – it won't take a minute."

"No." She said it firmly.

She heard the front room door slam and her father start to come up the stairs.

"Is Dermot coming?" she asked quickly, hoping that he was not.

"Yes, he's picking us up." Her mother was carefully pencilling a line on to her eyebrows.

She felt the slight twinge of nausea that usually accompanied the mention of Dermot's name these days. Her dad came into the room. Having just woken up, he looked old and tired, his face grey, his working clothes grimy and wrinkled.

For a moment she remembered the blue of Dermot's suit on the day she had seen him at Wood Green with her mother, his face shining with soap; no doubt if she had been close enough she would have smelt his aftershave and the faint hint of tobacco that usually surrounded him.

She gave her dad a hug as she went out of the room and he laughed and said, "What was that for?"

They got to the Excelsior at about eight thirty. Ann looked round for Rosie, but it was impossible to see if she and her family were there or not. The place was packed; there seemed to be thousands of people.

It was a massive hall and was decorated to look like a south sea island set from a Hollywood film. It was a funny place to have a St Patrick's Day celebration. The dance floor was in semi-darkness and looked as big as a field, and there was a forest of small tables that surrounded it, each with a lamp in the shape of a palm tree. People were sitting around talking, their voices swept away by the surging trombones and clarionettes of The Dublin Showband. An unmanned disco sat forlornly to the side of the band.

It was exactly the sort of music Ann hated, but it was a night out and Rosie had said that Tony might come (with Patricia).

Ann watched as a number of older people joined hands and stood still on the dance floor waiting for the music to start.

"And it's a Foxtrot!" The words came through the amplifiers.

The couples stood facing each other and were like kids in a game of musical statues waiting to start moving again. The music came, it seemed from nowhere. The dancers moved off round the floor, following some indeterminate pattern, taking two steps this way and then changing direction and taking three steps another. The man was always facing the front and the woman always moving backwards unaware of where she was being led or what was likely to happen to her.

Ann remembered her dad's cups for dancing on the sideboard in the flats and the way he'd taught her some ballroom steps when she had been much younger, when they had been regulars at the Irish Centre.

At the time she'd loved it when he said to her, "Would you care to dance?"

She'd got up, smoothing down the skirt of whatever dress she'd been wearing, smiling around in embarrassment and sighing deeply as though it were a chore and she was only doing it to please him.

They'd stood rigidly across from each other until the music started, she staring at his chest, his arms bent slightly because hers weren't long enough to reach. Then they would glide off, he half pulling, half dragging her three steps this way, two the other, a twirl under his arm a few steps on. The waltz was the easiest; one two three, one two three, one two three.

Her mum had even been quite good at it at one time, making herself brilliantly-coloured dresses with huge skirts and layers of petticoats.

The music stopped as abruptly as it had started. The dancers began to walk away from the floor when another blast came from the band.

She looked at her mum sitting waiting for her dad to bring the drinks back, a mildly bored expression on her face. She wondered what her mum had done with all the cups and medals and the old ballroom dresses. She saw her dad emerge out of the crowds, balancing a tray of drinks. Behind him came Dermot Duffy, his hands in his pockets, his shoulders moving shamelessly to the music.

Her dad handed her a bottle of lemonade with a straw in it (much to her annoyance, why couldn't she have had a glass?) and then tapped her mother on the shoulder and they both took a few steps onto the dance floor.

Ann rolled her eyes to no one in particular and sat down. A minute or so later Dermot joined her, his eyes on the dance floor, his fingers tapping out a rhythm on the table.

By the time she'd found Rosie and her family, Tony and Patricia had had a great row. He was sitting, long-faced, on one side of Mrs Kelly, and Patricia was looking intently round the dance floor on the other. Ann looked at her profile in the semi-darkness; her hair was in a pony tail, her long neck swivelling so that she could view the dancers, the band, the people standing round the edges. Ann noticed how her long triangular earrings swung rapidly and stabbed at her neck as she peered into different parts of the hall.

"Who said what?" Ann said

"Dunno. She did, I think. Dunno."

Rosie linked her arm and pulled her away from her mother and father and towards a large marble pillar the size of a fat tree.

"Here, look at this." Ann looked half-heartedly. She really wanted to stay close to Tony.

"Look!" Rosie thrust a small green bottle under

her nose. It was a bottle of gin the size of a half pint bottle of milk.

"Great." Ann said, not sure whether it was or not.

"We'll get some glasses and add a bit to our drinks all evening. It makes you feel good. I'm telling you."

A couple of moments later Rosie was pouring large sloshes of gin into two long glasses of lemonade. Ann took a sip as she watched Tony sitting to the side of his mother, his face like thunder, tapping his fingers deliberately out of time with the music as though in his head some quite different tune was playing. In front of him two of the younger Kellys looked as though they were wrestling on the carpet.

The gin tasted sharp. She shivered a little, and said it was very nice when Rosie looked at her.

"And it's a waltz!" the announcer said in the same tone that he had used before. Rosie's mother and father got up and, stepping across the children, walked towards the dance floor. It left a dark gap between Patricia and Tony, who were both looking away from each other.

Taking a more careful sip of her drink, Ann watched as a man walked up and stood in front of Patricia. He said something to her and her face broke into a smile. She got out of her seat and walked towards the dance floor with him. There was a spring in her step, and her earrings swung wildly about as she nodded and smiled.

"She's dancing with him! He must be twenty!"

Rosie said in a shrill whisper as she poured more gin into Ann's glass and her own.

Tony stood up abruptly.

"He'll hit him. You watch. He will." Rosie said nonchalantly, as though it was the most natural thing in the world, but he only looked out onto the dance floor for a minute or so and then stretching his arms into the air, as though he'd just got out of bed, he walked towards them. Ann took a gulp of her drink, which now tasted like a strong medicine she had once had. She held the bubbles in her mouth for a few seconds as she saw him come closer.

"He'll wait till it's over and then he'll hit him," Rosie said to herself.

But instead he walked up to Ann and said, "Wee Annie, would you care to dance?"

She didn't care that he only asked her to show Patricia. It meant something to her anyway. She wasn't in Patricia's league; she didn't have high up breasts that came to a point like a sideways pyramid, nor did she have lazy blonde hair and a permanently sulky expression. Nevertheless, he had asked her to dance.

It was enough. It made the evening for her.

In the darkness of the dance floor with other couples moving sideways, backwards, just going round in circles, she felt his arms tightly round her and her head felt heavy and the taste of the bubbles were in her mouth from the drink.

Over his shoulder she could see Patricia dancing closely with the man, and as they steered round the small area that they were dancing in, she felt Tony's hands moving up and down her back.

He lifted up his head for a moment and she thought he was going to say something to her and she moved her head in order to face him. But instead of speaking he kissed her on the mouth, gently at first, and because she wasn't expecting it their teeth scraped together. She felt his hand on the back of her neck steering her head and then he kissed her much harder. Her eyes were opened in surprise and she was about to shut them when she saw her mother's frock and Dermot's blue suit glide by.

The kiss faded into the background as the swirls on her mother's dress seemed to mingle with misty lights that moved round the floor. Where was her dad? Did he know that Dermot and her mum were dancing. Did he?

The music stopped abruptly and dozens of lights blazed onto the dancefloor. The kiss had also stopped. She had lost it somehow in the middle of seeing her mother and Dermot.

"Have your tickets ready for the buffet. I thank you," a voice from the stage said.

"Thank you," she said it stiffly. How could she have let the kiss slip away from her like that? How could she? She turned round and walked towards Rosie, a mild dizziness enveloping her.

"Fancy drinking gin, gerl." Dermot turned round from the driving seat and peered into the back of the car.

Her mother was sitting beside her, her face a picture of fury. Her dad was silent in the front.

The vomit stains on her skirt made the car smell even though the back window was open; Ann could feel the cold March wind cutting into her face. It was her punishment. Her skin felt chapped, but she was afraid to ask them to shut it.

"Now, don't be too hard on the gerl, Maureen."

Why was he always talking to her mum? He was supposed to be her dad's friend.

"We all have a bad time with our first drink." Dermot was the only one in the car who was laughing.

It was all very well for him to joke. Her parents might even nod and smile but there would be trouble when he dropped them home.

She turned her face into the chill breeze, parting her lips so that the sharp cold would take away the taste of the vomit. She should have stopped drinking after dancing with Tony. It had been silly for her and Rosie to try and finish the bottle between them.

But Tony Kelly had kissed her (not that she remembered much about it). He could have just danced with her, that would have made the point to Patricia. He had kissed her as well.

That had been something to celebrate.

CHAPTER TEN

"If only you hadn't brought that bloody gin to the Excelsior," Ann said to Rosie, as they stood at the school gates, "I wouldn't be in so much trouble now."

"I never forced you to drink it." Rosie threw a look over at Patricia who was waiting by a tree at the edge of the kerb.

"What's she doing here?" Ann said, looking resentfully at Patricia's hair which was blowing like yellow thread in the breeze.

"I never forced your mouth open and poured it down your throat." Rosie laughed in Patricia's direction as though involving her in some way.

Since Patricia had broken up with Tony she had taken to waiting for Rosie by the school gates every now and then. She always looked dolled up, even in her upper sixth uniform. She rarely looked at or spoke to Ann, but that wasn't unusual for sixth-formers. Rosie was in a privileged position.

"Anyway, if it hadn't been that, it would have

been something else. Your mum don't like me," she said, and Ann had no answer. It was true, but then there weren't many things that her mum did like these days.

Ann watched dismally as Rosie and Patricia walked off up the road towards the bus stop. In the distance she could hear their animated chatter.

She sat down on a wall near her own bus stop. What were they talking about? She idly pulled at a loose thread on her skirt and watched as the hem came away.

Ann's mother said she had to stay in for a month. She had to do without pocket money, do without new clothes. She found herself watching all the soap operas, the news, even the gardening programmes.

She wasn't allowed to have out of school contact with Rosie.

Her mother blamed the gin on Rose Kelly, and even though it had been Rosie who'd got the gin, Ann felt it an injustice that she had been automatically blamed for it. Her mother took to calling her "The Ever So Fantastic Miss Rose Kelly", and sneeringly brought Rosie's parents into every conversation that she had.

One morning Ann asked whether she could go and watch an after-school netball match. Her mother said, "I'm sure Mr and Mrs Kelly let their daughter roam the streets after school every afternoon, but I'm afraid we don't run to that. No, we don't."

Later she asked if she could have a new pair of

tights and with her fingers showed inch wide ladders and gaping holes in the toes of her one pair.

"I'm sure Mr and Mrs Kelly buy dozens of pairs of tights for their daughter but your father and I can only afford one."

Her mother's words were curt and crisp, as though she was talking to a shop assistant who had just upset her. Ann looked over at her dad who was rubbing a piece of sandpaper lethargically over the skirting board, his head lifting now and then to look at his wife.

"But then there's not much we can afford these days." Her mother threw the comment like a lasso in her dad's direction and walked out of the door.

Sometimes Ann wished her mother would go away and leave them. She was so miserable and sharp about everything. If her dad was sitting watching TV, his face still grimy after his day's work, she'd tut loudly, and go on about him bringing the building site into the front room; if he was upstairs washing himself in the bathroom she'd complain about the ensuing muck that would surround the basin after he had finished.

We'd be better off on our own, Ann thought, lying down on her bed, listening to her records.

But the thought of her mum actually going made Ann sit up with shock. In her head she saw her mother walking up the street, her red high heels clicking and scraping along the pavement, a battered brown suitcase in one hand full of perm curlers and dress patterns and matching earrings and necklaces. She shook her head. Whenever she let herself think of this she ended up with such a sense of panic that she almost had to put her head between her knees to steady herself.

"Here," her mother came into her bedroom one afternoon. "Three pairs for a pound. It would've been a sin to let them go." She threw the tights into the middle of the bed and walked out. Ann was left with the scent of her perfume in the room.

On the last day of term Ann and Rosie were sitting on the school wall, humming. They watched lazily as the buses they should have been on stopped, filled up with dark blue uniforms and then moved heavily on, their engines making great gasping sounds as they pulled away from the kerb. Ann stopped humming for a moment and watched the buses with a mild depression. One of them would take her home, back to her mum and dad's silences.

Rosie continued to hum quietly as though she hadn't a care in the world. It was as if they'd been out on a picnic and it was pleasure boats of holiday-makers they were watching come and go, not dusty red buses full of sweaty, fed-up people.

Eventually Rosie said, "Tony gave me another book, *Broken Promises*. It's good but I can't take it to Dublin with me." She searched through her bag and gave it to Ann. Excitement broke through the gathering gloom as she thought of going up to her room and nestling down on the bed to read about the comings and goings of people who made Broken Promises. The fact that Tony had already read it gave her added pleasure; it was like going somewhere that he had been, experiencing things that he had already done.

A knocking broke into her thoughts, and she and Rosie both looked round to the school building at the same time. At one of the windows they could see two of the nuns making signals with their hands. They seemed to be standing on tables because they were completely visible, their flowing skirts, their jumbo rosary beads and their policeman's shoes.

It was greatly frowned on for girls to hang around after school. They were meant to go straight home.

Both Ann and Rosie looked blankly at the two nuns who were waving their arms about frantically. Ann looked at Rosie, her eyes shining with glee. Rosie looked all around. Eventually she shrugged, her face a picture of innocent bewilderment.

By this time, one of the nuns had her hands on her hips in exasperation and Ann and Rosie slowly sat down again. It was like a peculiar game of charades. They couldn't hear what was being said to them. It wasn't their fault if they couldn't understand what they were supposed to do.

Looking back, Ann saw the nuns disappear from the window.

"How long do you think it'll take them?" Rosie said.

Ann sighed, blowing slowly through her teeth. "Let me see, along the corridor, down the stairs, through the dining hall, out of the cloakrooms, into the batmobile and up the drive – about a minute."

They both looked at their watches with delight

and with a sudden movement both girls were up off the wall and walking in opposite directions.

"See you!"

"In Gotham City," they both shouted, and ran off to the bus stop.

The Easter holidays descended amid palms and Stations of the Cross and Easter eggs. Rosie went to Ireland with her mother and younger brothers and sisters.

Ann sat in her room and thought of Tony Kelly and Dermot.

She was glad she hadn't said anything to Rosie about the kiss. Rosie would have said "Yuk", the way that sisters and brothers seemed to talk of each other, and it would have spoilt the reverie she was in.

She sat in her room among crumpled silver paper and pieces of uneaten curled chocolate and tried to recreate the kiss in her mind.

The trouble was that she wasn't sure she had experienced any feeling as such; at the point of whatever ecstasy was supposed to accompany a kiss she had seen her mother and Dermot waltzing past. Instead of her eyes closing she had been wide-eyed, her gaze following the couple moving gently back and forward on the dance floor. The lights had come on unexpectedly, and the dance and the kiss had stopped.

Whenever she tried to think of her own kiss, a picture of her mother's red lips moving slowly towards Dermot came into her mind. Had she seen this happen? Had Dermot really kissed her mother on the dance floor, there in front of her dad? She couldn't really say for sure. In her mind it seemed as though he had.

And her own kiss — was that real? She occasionally brushed her fingers across her lips as though feeling for it there.

Perhaps she had imagined it all.

CHAPTER ELEVEN

It was the last Saturday in May when Ann and Rosie decided to follow Maureen O'Brien.

Her dad was going to be working all weekend and the plan had been for Ann and her mum to go and see Our Mary who lived in Greenford.

Our Mary was her mother's older sister and her mother never spoke about her without using this title. She never said Mary did this or Mary did that. She was always Our Mary even when the sentence didn't require the pronoun. Ann always supposed that she had her reasons; like the way she insisted on talking about Dermot Duffy and not just Dermot.

Going to Greenford was a real expedition. They had to get two buses and then a tube journey that seemed to take as long as the Orient Express and then another bus. Ann quite enjoyed the stop go, stop go feel of the tube but she was humpy and heard herself say, "Do we have to?" when her mother told her they were going.

Ann liked Our Mary; she also liked her twin

cousins who were about eighteen months older than she and were always telling her dirty stories; but her shoulders were stiffly rounded and she said, "They're stuck up anyway, them two. They talk funny."

She even liked the dozens of tiny sandwiches and the small chocolate marshmallows that Our Mary got from Marks & Spencer's for when they came. She knew as she said it she'd regret her mood. "It's boring going up there!"

Finally her mother, who had been ironing, pointed her finger in mid-air and said, "Look, if you don't want to come, that's fine by me. You can stay with the Ever So Fantastic Miss Rose Kelly. Let Mr and Mrs Kelly feed you and look after you. I'll go and see Our Mary on my own. I'll have a better time without your long humpy face dragging behind me."

"What've I said?" Ann put her hand on her chest as though the finger had been directed there and she had been bruised. "What've I said?"

"Never you mind, Miss. Never you mind." Her mother wound the flex of the iron round its handle like a practised murderer, pulling tight with each circumference. The iron groaned as she put it down in the corner.

"I'll go by myself. I'll buy a magazine, I'll buy some sweets and I'll sit on the tube and enjoy my own company. Never you mind."

Later that morning, lying on her bed brooding on her mother's awkwardness, she heard the phone ring. The ring stopped and she could hear her mother's voice.

"Yes?"

There was a long silence and she could hear a couple of "um"s. Eventually she heard,

"Well, never mind. There's no problem. I've loads to do anyway. Look after yourself. I'll ring you in a week or so."

After reading her magazines over again, Ann got up and went downstairs. Her mother was sitting at the kitchen table, putting heated rollers in her hair.

"Who was on the phone?"

"No one," her mother said. "No one that you'd know."

"What's happening this afternoon then?" she said, sure that it had been Our Mary on the phone cancelling their visit.

"I'm away to Our Mary's. I've told you. You can please yourself. You're always saying you want some freedom. Well there, you've got it. I'll be back about sevenish. Your dad'll be back from work this afternoon sometime. Make sure you're back home before me. You know what he's like."

Rosie had been the one who'd come up with the idea.

"She's meeting HIM," she said. "Why don't we follow her and catch her red-handed?"

As they were getting into disguise, Ann felt a sudden deep dragging feeling of guilt. It was her mum they were going to catch red-handed.

Her mum, who only the other day had taken

her to Wood Green to try on jackets like the one Patricia had. She'd even hinted that she might buy her one.

Her mum, who had helped her to get money out of her dad at Christmas for a new wardrobe and chest of drawers for her bedroom.

Her mum, who always came up to school looking about twenty, who made her proud when everyone said, "Is that your mum?" with disbelief.

"It's no good disguising ourselves with wigs or make-up or nothing," Rosie said. "She'd be sure to spot us. We need to throw her off completely by being something that we couldn't possibly be."

Ann looked around at Rosie's empty front room. At least her family weren't here to watch them.

"Something that she would never ever expect us to be . . ." Rosie's face was set in concentration.

They got the cushions from Rosie's front room and tied them on to their middles with old tights. Rosie got her school mac and buttoned it up over the lump, then she got an old mac of her mother's for Ann.

They tied headscarves over their hair and Rosie got her sister's glasses out of a drawer in the kitchen, small lavender frames with tiny wings at the side; her dad's reading glasses they found beside the telly.

In the mirror they saw two young pregnant girls in glasses and headscarves.

"She won't even look, see. It would be the last way she would expect to see you or me."

Rosie's face was beaming, and she kept turning

round and looking admiringly in the mirror as though it was a brand new outfit she was wearing.

Ann sneered. Since Rosie had become a friend of Patricia's she had become very interested in the way she looked. She'd started to iron her clothes with great care and was always stopping along the street to look at herself in shop windows.

Looking at her own reflection, Ann saw a plain, round-shouldered girl with an uneven lump in the front of her coat.

She began to feel anger towards Rosie for enjoying it, for taking delight in what they were doing. She wanted to say something cutting, something that summed up all her frustrations. In her mind, though, it was her mum she was telling off. But when she imagined herself speaking, it was Patricia she was addressing, not her mum at all.

In the end she just said, "You look stupid!" and Rosie laughed.

Ann put her hands deep into the pocket of the mac and gingerly followed Rosie out of the house. She fervently hoped that Tony wouldn't be coming home for his lunch at that very minute.

They stood out as they walked along the street because it was hot and breezy and they had long coats on. A couple of older women looked after them as they walked past. Ann felt distinctly uncomfortable and she watched as Rosie held her back and leant against garden walls the way she'd seen pregnant women do. Ann rounded her shoulders and hoped no one would see her.

Somewhere inside, behind the fake lump, Ann

was afraid. It was one thing thinking her mother might be having an affair, it was another thing actually following her. What if they found it out today? What if they walked into her mum and Dermot kissing or holding hands? Then she'd be obliged to tell her dad.

Rosie decided that they would wait on the High Road near the top of Ann's street. There was a bench there, obscured by a bus shelter a few yards to the right. There were a couple of overgrown bushes on the edge of the pavement and four lanes of traffic to look across.

"There's no way that she'll even see us through this, let alone recognize us!" Rosie talked about Ann's mum as though she was just some stranger that they were following, a "suspect".

They sat down on the bench, Rosie chattering excitedly; two expectant mums enjoying a rest.

"Did you see that woman on the bus?" Rosie said. "She was looking at my hand for my wedding ring. She probably thinks I'm from the Unmarried Mother's Home." Rosie was chuckling. Ann felt her temper rising. She looked sideways at her friend, it was all a game for her. It wasn't her mum and dad that were involved.

Her and her gigantic family; the old lady who lived in a shoe. Her mum and her dad, their dozens of relations in Ireland, the six kids. It was all so solid. Just then, Ann's own family, her mum, dad and her, seemed tiny and fragile in comparison. It wouldn't take much to smash it, she thought. She saw a family photograph in her head that had been broken three ways, the cracks in the glass brittle and sharp, the paper underneath torn roughly, without care, without thought.

"Here she is!" Rosie said.

Patting down her fringe and partly covering her face with her hand, Ann looked across the High Road and saw her mother walking out of their street. She was wearing her newest dress, the one she had spent hours sewing the previous week. Ann felt a lump in her throat. She wanted to reach over and say to Rosie, "Let's leave it", but Rosie had already got up off the bench and was saying, "Come on, come on."

Ann stood up and took Rosie's dad's glasses off. She wanted to stop. This was no game, this was her family they were playing with. Out of the corner of her eye she saw that a car had stopped. It was bibbing its horn just yards away from her.

"She's there, look, a bit away from the bus stop," Rosie hissed back at her. "She's probably waiting for someone to pick her up. I bet HE'S picking her up. Look!"

But Ann couldn't look. The bibbing in her head was getting louder and she thought for a moment that she was becoming ill. The heat of her disguise became oppressive and she pushed the headscarf off her head and began to unbutton the coat. The cushion seemed to be growing in size, puffing up and pushing at the walls of her chest. She pulled at the tights, and in a moment the cushion was under her arm and the coat was hanging loose.

She glanced round at the bibbing and saw with

a shock that it was her dad's car, and that he was sitting grinning at her, his hands on the wheel, his back to where her mother was standing.

In panic, she turned her head and looked again at her mother, who was facing away from them looking up the road in search of something (she was near a bus stop; maybe she waiting for a bus take her to the tube and then to Our Mary's in Greenford).

She looked with dismay towards Rosie, who was peering round the side of the bus shelter like a detective in a cartoon, waiting to see Dermot's car drive up and whisk her mother off.

And here was her dad, having seen straight through her disguise, sitting laughing in his car at his little girl playing dressing up games, unaware that behind his back his wife was standing on the other side of the road, very probably waiting for her secret lover.

She sat back down on the bench in fright. Any minute now, Dermot would drive up the road and pick her mother up, and all her dad had to do was turn round or look in his rear view mirror and he would see.

What had she done? If she hadn't been standing here, playing silly detective games, her dad wouldn't have stopped.

Hours seemed to pass as she looked helplessly from Rosie to her dad to her mum and back to Rosie.

If they got to the car quickly and asked him for a lift somewhere, he would drive off and not see anything.

But she had to get up off the bench, get Rosie away from behind the bus shelter and into her dad's car, without him turning round or her mother suddenly noticing his car or them across the traffic. Her legs began to shake and she thought for an awful moment that she was not going to be able to get up, that her legs would flap under her, useless, like a rag doll.

Looking towards her dad's car, she saw that he had taken his hands off the wheel and was moving about, as if he were getting ready to get out of the car and come over to her.

In a flash, she stood up and walked towards Rosie and pulled the arm of her coat. Across the road, her mother was pacing up and down and seemed miles away. She hadn't noticed them at all.

"Quick, into my dad's car. Quick."

Rosie let a silent gasp and in two or three strides was in the back of Ann's dad's car.

"Hello, Mr O'Brien," she said.

"You're looking a bit fat there, Rosemary," he said manoeuvring a small tin of tobacco onto the dashboard behind the steering wheel.

"Her name's Rosie, Dad," Ann said, getting into the front seat. "We're doing some drama homework. It's called role play. Can you give us a lift down Turnpike Lane? We're in ever such a hurry."

"I'm seeing Dermot at the betting shop. Will West Green Road do?"

"Fine," Ann said. *He was meeting Dermot.*

The car moved away from the kerb and, glancing

back round, Ann saw her mother still waiting by the side of the road. Leaning back on the car seat, ignoring Rosie's conspiratorial wink, she felt a heavy sadness for both of them. She pictured her mum standing there for hours and hours as the traffic whizzed indifferently past. Her dad she saw leaning against the counter of the betting shop, his special betting pencil behind his ear, checking his watch and the clock and glancing up each time the door opened.

One of them is going to be disappointed this afternoon, she thought.

CHAPTER TWELVE

At the end of June there was a heatwave. Ann and Rosie sat in their shorts, sucking lollies outside Wood Green Shopping City.

"We really ought to think about getting Saturday jobs," Rosie said between long slurps.

"Um . . ." Ann had gone into a hairdresser's a couple of days previously to ask if they needed anyone. She'd stood waiting for a few moments but the smell of lacquer and the heat of the driers and the bored faces of the girls had made her go out again without saying anything.

"Pat works in Marks & Spencer's. There's a waiting list there."

"Um . . ." Ann said. Rosie had abbreviated Patricia's name and was always mentioning her in conversations. "What were you saying about going to St John's tomorrow?" Ann changed the subject.

"Oh . . ." Rosie was down to the last mouthful of the lolly and seemed to have the whole stick sideways in her mouth. "You could," she said, swivelling it so that it looked like a flat cigarette, "you could come to mass at St John's. For a change."

"It's a long way," Ann said, thinking of two buses and the walk.

"All the sixth-formers from the college go there for mass. I seen them."

Ann pictured rows of boys in brown jackets with yellow piping. Tony Kelly would probably be there. She hadn't seen him properly since St Patrick's night. The three or four times she'd been round Rosie's he'd not been in. She'd caught sight of him once going round the corner as she'd turned into Rosie's street, and once she'd heard music from his bedroom as she'd passed on her way to the toilet.

It seemed like years since she'd seen him. "I'll call for you about half ten," she said decisively.

When Ann got home that afternoon her dad was standing buttering bread at the kitchen table.

He nodded curtly at her but there was no smile on his face.

"I told you. I told you. I don't want you working there. I don't want you going near there." He was pointing a buttery knife into the air but he was looking straight at the loaf of bread on the table.

Her mum was sitting on a high stool in her bikini top and shorts. "I only went to Jackson's to see the girls. I didn't know he was going to ask me to go back."

"We agreed, before we moved to this house, we agreed."

"That was before the bills started to come in."

"There's other jobs!" Her dad folded the bread over in two, took a bite and walked out of the door.

"But it's all right for you to go in there!" Her mum's voice rose and she got off the stool. She looked at Ann and, picking up the buttery knife and dropping it into the sink, said quietly, "It's all right for him."

Ann braced herself as the front door slammed, and then went up to her room.

The next day Ann found herself in a strange church, sitting in a pew by herself. Across the aisle was a large red-faced woman who was holding her rosary as though it was a skein of wool that someone else was rolling up for her. Other people in front and behind her were kneeling, but she just sat on the very edge of the seat, her knees slanted down to the ground.

She had told Rosie she would call for her. Going to mass at St John's had been Rosie's idea in the first place. It was hot and sweaty and she'd walked all the way along White Hart Lane to knock for her and she'd been out.

"She's over at Patricia's," Mrs Kelly had said. "The girl rang last night in tears and our Rose got her things and went over. She's a bit depressed I think, because of the boy. He'll have nothing to do with her." Mrs Kelly had been standing at her front door holding a baby's sock in one hand and a grey knee-length one in the other. Ann had stood dismally while she spoke and watched as she put one sock on top of the other and smoothed them both down, over and over, as though determined to make a pair of them.

"I'm telling you this is hot, Annie," Mrs Kelly had said, watching one of the smaller children crawling about in the uneven grass of the front garden.

Ann had turned away. "I'll go on, then."

"Mind this air?" Mrs Kelly had said, waving the socks about, "I'm telling you, you could cut it with a knife and fork."

In the church, Ann sat back on her seat as people from other pews edged by to go up for communion. She watched as people knelt down at the front altar and a very old priest with a shock of white hair moved falteringly along, giving each a round piece of wafer.

She gazed round the church at the grey uneven walls and the vivid stained glass windows. On the wall at the end of her pew was one of the stations of the cross. It was a crumbling mosaic and the faces were sharp and full of angles. The last time she had been in a church this old had been at her uncle's funeral some eighteen months or so ago after he had been killed in a car crash.

For a moment, a picture of her mum and dad and her came into her mind, as they had been, at that funeral. They were in the car and they were all laughing at something. They were following the cortège to the cemetery, and her dad was making jokes. For some reason her mum was sitting in the back with her. She was wearing a black cotton dress that she'd sewn up on the day her uncle had died and a small back cloche hat with black netting that came down over her eyes.

Her dad said that her uncle would have wanted them to laugh, that he had always laughed at people's funerals, that it was better to remember people with joy than with sorrow.

Ann could remember sitting in the back seat of their car and amid the laughter feeling an intense longing whenever she looked at her mum or dad. It came to her that they too were old, that they too, like her uncle, could just suddenly die. Her mum could walk out of the front door one day to do some shopping and never come back. Her dad might stumble on a slippery piece of steel and then they'd never again wait for him to come in at night so that they could all eat their tea together

There, in that strange church, Ann had that feeling again. She thought of her dad's chair empty, his stool where he put his feet tidied away to some other room and his bingo and betting pencils all in a box on top of the wardrobe. Her view became blurred as she felt her tears coming and she remembered why her mother was in the back seat of the car with her on that day. Dermot was in the front seat. The four of them had gone to the funeral.

Her dad and mum; her mum and Dermot; Dermot and Maureen.

It was Rosie's and Patricia's fault that she felt like this. If Rosie had been here like she said, she wouldn't be nearly in tears in front of everyone.

Patricia Hogan, who had suddenly become Rosie's

best friend, who gave her clothes and bits of make-up, who phoned her up at home and spoke for ages about the boys she was going out with.

Rosie had let her down again; she'd forgotten her in the excitement of a summons from Patricia.

The communion was over and Ann took some deep breaths of the cool dark church air. Looking up towards the balcony, she caught sight of Tony Kelly. He smiled at her.

She waved back, her melancholy dissolving, the gloom in her stomach transforming into a jittery delight. She smoothed her skirt down and started to comb through her hair with her fingers.

He was waiting in the crowds outside.

"Well, Ann, how are you?" he said.

"Fine." In some writing book in her head she noted that he had called her "Ann" for the first time and not "Wee Annie".

"Where's the villain?" he said. He'd not even noticed that Rosie hadn't been home the previous evening.

"Dunno."

After a moment's silence, he said, "Fancy coming round Wednesday afternoon? We could listen to some records."

He was asking her for a date.

"You could look at my library. I know you like reading." He laughed. It wasn't exactly a date he was asking her on. They weren't going out anywhere.

She was struck with silence. It was as if he'd just asked her to walk to Kilimanjaro. Her tongue felt as though it was stuck to her palate. If she didn't answer soon he would think she didn't want to.

"Wednesday?" She eventually said as though it was simply the day that was making her pause, as though any other day would have been better.

"Me mum goes out Wednesday."

They'd be in the house on their own. She would have to bunk off. To lie to her mum. She'd have to lie to Rosie.

In the distance she could see Rosie and Patricia half walking and half running up the road, towards the church. She had probably remembered this morning that Ann was going to call for her. She had even dragged Patricia along.

"Wednesday's fine," Ann said watching them as they came closer.

"About two?"

"See you then," she said, and walked briskly off past Tony, past Patricia and past Rosie.

On the bus on the way home she felt good. Rosie had let her down for the last time.

PART FOUR

Discoveries

At least she didn't have nightmares.

If Ann had had nightmares about Rosie's death then she could have tossed violently about in her bed and woken up in a mist of perspiration and cries, and her mother or father would have rushed to her bedside – like they did in the films.

But she didn't have nightmares. She hadn't dreamt about it at all. Her sleep was like jumbled-up films. Her mum and dad wandered in and out of them as well as Rosie and Tony and a couple of other people.

Sometimes there were bits of them that slipped into a sharp focus and were like a mirror of life. Her mum and dad would be acting like mums and dads did and Rosie would call for her to go out to play, and when she came she'd have some kind of toy with her, a skipping rope or a couple of racquets and a ball. Ann would laugh and begin to say that they were too old to be playing games but there'd be some kind of happiness swimming around inside her chest. Even in the dream she could feel it, the way she felt when she was a young child and had just bought a quarter of sherbet lemons on her way to the pictures.

Her eyes would open and she would be lying in the semi-darkness of her own bedroom, a dull light forcing its way through the curtain and the sounds of birds' squawking cries piercing the quiet of the room.

In a second the delight of the dream would disappear and be replaced by the familiar heaviness that she was used to carrying around with her.

On the morning that Miss Martin was due to come and see her, she had been thinking about the few minutes just before the accident. She peered vacantly into the darkness of her room and tried to see if she could visualize herself and Rosie walking along the road, as though she were sitting far above in the clouds watching down – like God.

She saw them walking, talking animatedly and then Rosie angrily striding out in front for a few seconds, then stopping and turning round. She saw herself turn away and walk towards the edge of the pavement and Rosie pulling her back round and grabbing her hands.

The two girls then began to turn in slow motion; holding hands, they spun round and round like children playing in a park.

Ann sat up and concentrated. Where had the juggernaut come from? Behind her? The other way?

From round the corner? She was sure it hadn't been there when she'd looked, when she'd turned for the road. It had appeared like a ghost.

She wanted to see if she could recreate the exact moment when Rosie went under, if she could see what she had been doing, if she could have stopped it. But all she could hear was the screech of the brakes.

She stopped being God and was back on the pavement again looking at the clouds of dust that had been set off by the wheels of the lorry, wondering where Rosie had gone. For a brief moment she thought that Rosie had finally left her and gone to Patricia for good. And then she saw the driver running from the lorry.

She felt sick for a minute, bile rising in her throat, and she lay back down on her pillow. Instead of forgetting it, instead of the pain receding, she was beginning to feel physically sick now whenever she thought of it.

Why had she told Miss Martin that she had pushed Rosie? She would never have pushed Rosie. Rosie was the best friend she had ever had.

When she was little she used to say that her mum was her best friend and that she was going to marry her dad.

She stopped and thought about Dermot Duffy. Whenever she thought about her mum and dad his name would come into her head a few seconds later.

He had gone to Ireland to see his fiancée, her mother said. She had had appendicitis, her mother said. It had all been a last minute thing. He'd got a telegram and had had to rush for the train. It was just like Dermot Duffy, he hadn't even had a suitcase he could take, her mother said. She had not trusted him to get on the train on time so she'd gone down to Euston with him.

Men! They needed looking after like children.

Her mum had lent him a suitcase.

Her mum had gone with him to Euston so that he wouldn't miss the train.

She'd looked closely at her mum's face to see if it was the truth, if there was a flicker of uneasiness about her eyebrows or some anxious lines on her forehead.

Later, when her mum had been talking about Dermot's fiancée and her job as a nurse, Ann had looked for some sadness in her eyes, some bitterness in the way she held her mouth, but there was none.

Perhaps it was all over. Maybe it would be all right and they would stay like a family.

It was too late for her, though; too late to put right the thing that she had done.

She hadn't pushed Rosie, but she had killed her, only she knew that.

But at least she didn't have nightmares.

It wasn't strictly part of Kate Martin's job to visit girls at home, but since Ann hadn't been to school for over a week she decided that it was the only way that she could talk to her and sort out this business about Rose Kelly's death.

135

"How are you, Ann?" Kate said, sitting on the O'Brien's settee.

"She's been a bit sick this week, vomiting and stuff. It'll be something she ate." Kate heard Mrs O'Brien's voice from the other room alongside the clinking sound of cups and teaspoons.

Later when she'd finished her tea and chatted for a while, Kate realized that Mrs O'Brien was going to stay, that she wasn't going to be able to talk to Ann on her own. She decided to raise the subject anyway. She knew that Sister Dominic wouldn't like it. She knew that her head teacher hadn't wanted her to come at all.

"What goes on at home is not our affair, Kate," she'd said, "it's up to the parents to deal with problems of an ... an ..." For a second Sister Dominic had been stuck for words.

"Emotional?" Kate had offered.

"Emotional nature," she'd said, as though that very word had just popped into her head. "School is for education, my dear Kate. Home and its problems, that's not an area that we should get into. After all, Mr and Mrs Kelly are the ones we should be praying for. They're the ones who have lost in all this."

But apart from making Kate feel righteous, prayers had never actually changed anything that she had been aware of. Fifteen-year-old girls still were run over and were killed; their mothers and fathers wept into their pillows every night until memory lessened its grip and let them fall into sleep.

Prayers didn't help a fifteen-year-old girl who thought she was to blame for her friend's death.

Kate looked at Ann.

"Just over a week ago, Ann, you made it clear to me that you'd remembered something new about Rose Kelly's death?"

"Ann?" Mrs O'Brien said, a puzzled expression on her face.

"You were too upset to go into the details but you said you'd come back and see me the next day and explain. You haven't been back in school since."

Kate stared at Ann for a few moments.

"What was it that you wanted to say?"

"I . . . I . . ." Ann seemed to sit up to attention before she spoke. She looked at Kate and then towards her mother.

"Ann?" Mrs O'Brien looked over at her daughter and the girl folded her arms and rounded her shoulders. She seemed to visibly shrink into the seat.

"I sometimes think . . . you know . . . that I was to blame . . . I was there . . . I could perhaps have stopped her . . ." Ann was hugging herself and her voice was breaking.

Kate pursed her lips. It hadn't been a good idea to come. The girl wasn't going to say anything in front of her mother. How could she have been so stupid to think she would?

Mrs O'Brien went over and sat by her daughter. "She's not at all well, Miss Martin. Does she have to go through these questions again? What is the point? The girl's dead. What possible good can it do? Nothing can bring the girl back."

Just then the phone rang from out in the hall.

"Excuse me," Mrs O'Brien said stiffly. She walked reluctantly away from her daughter and out of the door.

When she had gone, Kate decided on one last try.

"Ann, I think there's something you're not telling us, something that relates to the accident, something you're afraid to say." She took a piece of paper from her bag and began to write on it. "Here's my phone number. If you want to talk I promise it won't go any further – if you don't want it to. Not your parents, not Sister Dominic, no one. I promise. Here – take it."

Ann took the piece of paper just as Mrs O'Brien came back into the room. "Excuse me", she said again. "Look, Miss Martin, the whole thing's been a shock for everyone. Ann's father and me, we think it's better to try and forget it. I know you mean well, but Ann's just a bit off colour at the moment. It's natural. She lost her friend. I think it would be better if you let the whole thing drop. Ann will probably go back to school next Monday."

Kate smiled at Mrs O'Brien. "I'm really sorry to have troubled you. It's a distressing business for everyone. I hope you're better soon, Ann."

Getting into her car, Kate sat back and thought, what if I'm wrong? What if it's all the hysterics of a teenage girl? If Sister Dominic is right? Kate visualized the nun striding down a corridor of the school towards her, her face pinched, her black garments swinging out behind her, her hands rolling her sleeves up as though she were about to engage in a fist fight.

138

Kate turned the key in the ignition. She noticed for a second her cream rosary beads that hung down from her rear view mirror. They'd hung there for years, clattering against the glass of the window whenever she turned a corner or stopped suddenly. They'd become like part of the car itself, so much so that she rarely noticed them there, like the tiny vial of holy water in her mother's hall.

They were just coloured stone and metal after all. With her hand she unhooked them gently from the mirror and shut them into her glove compartment, started the car up and drove off.

Still sick some days later, Ann began to think about her periods.

Her thoughts had been triggered by a remark her mum had made one day after she'd been sick again in the bathroom basin.

Standing with a bottle of Domestos, her mum had kissed her lightly on the back of the head and said, "It's just as well you're not just being sick in the morning or else I'd be thinking you were pregnant."

She'd laughed and hummed to herself as she tipped some of the bleach into the sink and swilled it round with a flush of water from the tap.

"I expect that will be the first thing Dermot Duffy will do when he gets married – have a child. About time too!"

Her mum and dad had spoken to her on the night that Miss Martin had come round. They'd been holding hands and telling her about how Rosie wouldn't have wanted her to be upset like this and that Rosie was in heaven and she would see her again one day. She hadn't really been listening to what they said because she was watching their hands on the settee, their fingers entwined. Although Ann had seen her parents touching before, hugging or dancing, she had never seen them holding hands. Her dad had looked different, his face was pink and shiny as though someone had just given him a good wash, and he had changed out of his work clothes. Her mum was wearing a new skirt and top that she'd made. She didn't seem bothered that Dermot had gone, it was the opposite. She was relaxed, making jokes about Dermot Duffy meeting his fiancée of twelve years and not recognizing her.

Had she been right about her mum and Dermot? Had there been something between them?

She had seen them together at Wood Green; she had seen them kissing in the Excelsior. She was sure she had. A feeling of nausea, like a cloud, settled on her stomach.

She could barely eat and was sick a number of times over the next few days. Then her mum had made the remark about being pregnant.

It reminded her of the time eighteen months or so before, when she'd been waiting for her first ever period.

All her other friends in the flats had come on. Their chests had started to come into points and their mothers had bought them small lacy bras. They went in pairs to the small chemist's in the

140

next road and giggled wildly when they asked for "sanitarytowels", which they always said as though it was one word.

One or two of the older girls sneered at these juvenile displays by loudly asking for "Tampax" or "Lil-lets" with the nonchalance of someone buying a loaf of bread. Once outside they exhibited the attractive cellophane-covered packet for anybody who wanted to look. Ann had looked at the small, neat box of Tampax and was puzzled as to how it could have any relation to the large soft plastic packets of towels. She'd asked what it was, exactly, that you did with them; to her the tampons looked like fat cotton wool cigarettes. The others had just shrugged their shoulders and said, "Oh you know . . ."

She'd looked at her mum's packet of towels a couple of times. She'd had to get it out of the very back of the linen cupboard because it couldn't be anywhere that her dad might see it. Men, it seemed, had an aversion to viewing the outside of a packet of sanitary towels. It wasn't something they were to be subjected to.

Her mother came in while she'd been looking, and tutted loudly but not unkindly. She told her not to be so silly, to put it back, that she'd have a lifetime of the things, that she was time enough starting when she was seventeen.

But all her friends had started. She was nearly fourteen and beginning to worry that it would never happen. Someone told her of a woman who had never had a period and lived until she was in her sixties with a chest as flat as floorboards and long grey hairs growing out of her chin.

But then, after having a row with her mum about helping with the shopping one day, she sat herself in her dad's chair and started to read a book when she felt unusual dragging pains in her stomach and at the tops of her thighs. Her head felt heavy and she kept changing position in the chair.

She felt awkward and uncomfortable and her legs and stomach felt as though some imaginary thing was pulling and stretching at her muscles. There was no focus to the pain – it just seemed to be there; not bad enough to lie and cry about; not vague enough to forget about.

In the end she got up and went to the toilet.

The sight of blood should have shocked her, but it didn't. For a brief moment she was confused and then it dawned on her. The listlessness and the pains and the gathering gloom that she had felt seemed to fall away from her and she ran out of the flat and down the stairs into the street. It was then that she realized that she was looking for her mum; to tell her what had happened. She ran up the street and into the High Road. There were three or four shops that her mum usually went into and she ducked her head into each one, searching with her eyes for her mother.

For a couple of moments she felt a surge of disappointment as she thought she wasn't going to see her. If only she'd not been sulky and gone shopping in the first place! Then she saw her across the road, coming out of Tesco's, carrying two carrier bags full of shopping.

The road was clear and in a second she was across it and beside her.

"What's the matter?" her mum said, her forehead wrinkling in anticipation of some bad news.

"I've come on!" Ann didn't say it, she announced it.

Her mum laughed and then looked around. One or two women were walking past but were not looking at them.

"I've come on," Ann said again, with glee, quieter this time but looking her mum straight in the face.

The row was forgotten and her mum rolled her eyes.

"I don't know what you're so happy about," she said, smiling. "It's the start of a whole load of trouble." And she walked on, manoeuvring in and out of the other shoppers, slowly shaking her head.

The next day she bought Ann two bras, six pairs of knickers and some deodorant. In the same bag as the deodorant was a packet of painkillers.

Had it only been eighteen months ago? Had she been so excited over that? The pains and the headaches, the checking dates and wondering why, some months, nothing happened at all.

Eighteen months ago; so much had happened in that time. They had moved house. She had thought her mum and dad would split up over Dermot. She had met Rosie.

It was already ten weeks since Rosie had died.

She had met Tony Kelly.

And it was over twelve weeks since she had had a period.

CHAPTER THIRTEEN

The truth was that Ann did need Rosie.

The day after the break-up, Rosie sat apart from Ann in all lessons and on Tuesday Ann brought back three of Tony's books and dumped them onto the desk where Rosie was sitting. She looked up, and without any expression, took the books and put them straight into her bag. Ann felt an invisible door closing in her face. She turned and went back to her seat.

She missed her bitterly. Looking across the room and seeing Rosie chatting to other girls made her seethe with frustration. Ann responded by having loud, animated conversations with girls around her and she laughed exaggeratedly at their jokes.

When she saw Rosie talking to Patricia in the playground, her feelings turned to anger. She wanted to walk over and slap her silly face. She wished Patricia Hogan was dead.

When Ann had told her mother about it the previous evening, she just said, "What did you expect?" and then Ann felt worse, as though she'd betrayed Rosie by talking to her mum about it at all.

Rosie wasn't lonely, how could she be? She had her whole family to go home to; she had her new, older friend.

On Tuesday night Ann sat in her room and thought of the next day with Tony Kelly. It was the first time she'd had a chance to think it through. Not that she'd been busy, but her mind had been full of an imaginary picture of Rosie and Patricia sitting together on the bench in the playground, giggling, whispering, swapping books. It amazed her that she had almost forgotten about Tony in her preoccupation with her broken friendship.

It wouldn't be hard to slip out after lunch. She hadn't been off sick for a while, and it was months since that time when they had bunked off, when they had seen Dermot and her mother in the car.

She thought wistfully for a moment of how different everything would be now if she hadn't been at Wood Green that day, if she hadn't seen her mum with Dermot. She wouldn't have to worry every time her mum came in late or feel pity for her dad every time he winked at her mum.

She heard the front door slam and her father's voice shouting for her mother. She looked at her watch; it was half seven, her mother would be annoyed because he was so late.

What a pair they made. What a lot of trouble they were for her. Here she was on the eve of a big date and all she could think of was their problems.

She shook her head at herself and her lack of concentration. She had to think about Tony Kelly and the next day. She went across and sat in front of her dressing table mirror. What exactly were they going to do the next day? They could talk and listen to records but would that fill up two hours or so? She and Rosie never had any trouble filling up two hours. That afternoon when they'd both bunked off they'd chatted and talked, they'd sat on benches by the road and taken the mickey out of people. And then they'd gone back to Rosie's house and caught Tony and Patricia.

She had a picture in her head of Tony's room the day she had passed it when he and Patricia had been there. The rumpled bed, his school uniform hung neatly over the wooden chair. His shoes with the socks tucked in. The odd feeling it had given her to imagine what had happened there.

It was while she was thinking of these things that she heard the raised voices from downstairs.

There was a row. She got up and went over to the door of her room. The front room door was open and she could hear their voices.

"... I go out to have a bit of life. I don't want to be stuck here while you're at work most of the time. Jesus – I'm thirty-six not sixty-six ..."

"There's loads of jobs; Marks & Spencer's, Woolworths. They were looking for a welfare woman up the school, you told me yourself ..."

"I had a job. I was good at it. Jackson said I could have it back any time I liked ..."

Ann went quietly out onto the landing and sat on

the top stair. Her dad had been stripping wallpaper over the last couple of weeks and the whole wall looked like a giant map of an unknown world. With her thumb nail she started edging a corner of the yellowing paper off.

"I don't want you there. How do I know what you're doing?"

"What do you know? It's all in your frigging head. It's there, it's up there . . ."

"You're always dressing up. You're always doing your hair. It's not right. The place is full of blokes . . ."

"To look nice . . . You used to like it . . . You used to take care with how you looked. Look at you now. You're like an old man."

"I do a dirty job. I work for . . . To buy things. A house, to buy you a house. It's what you wanted. You plagued me night and day to move out of the flats. And now we're here, you're not happy."

Her dad's voice had lowered and Ann moved down the stairs a few steps and continued to pick at the wallpaper, peeling it gently away and then pulling long shredded strips, making rivers and islands of what was left.

"I thought this was what you wanted. Me and you and Ann. Our own house, a wee car, a bit of money in our pockets."

"It is."

There was silence.

"It was. But I don't want it on my own. I want company. I want someone to talk to. You're never here. I spend all day wandering around the house. I'm not allowed to do a job I liked. What am I supposed to do with myself? The child's never here, she's got her own life. What should I do? Tell me that. Sit on my arse?"

"You don't know what the blokes in the betting shop are like. You don't know how they talk . . ."

"And you do? And you know why? Because you're one of them. That's why you can't stand it."

A door banged and the voices moved away into the kitchen and Ann shuffled down the stairs on her bottom.

"I'll go to Our Mary's. Just for a while. Ann can come with me or she can stay here. I have to have time to think . . ."

"Do what you frigging like. There's no pleasing you."

Her dad's voice was hard. It was as though he was building a brick wall with every word.

Her mum was going to leave. She was going to take the bus and the tube and go to Our Mary's in Greenford. She was going to leave her dad on his own.

There'd be nobody to get him up in the morning or remind him to change his working shirt.

She could hear the sound of the telly being turned on and raucous canned laughter from some show or other.

"That's it, bury yourself in the telly. One day someone will come in here and find you covered in cobwebs."

"You think you're a girl again, that's your trouble. You better grow up, woman . . ."

And Ann heard the kitchen door slam.

She got off the stair and walked straight out of the front door and into the night.

She held the telephone receiver away from her face because it felt sticky; with her foot she held the door open because the cubicle smelt of urine.

"I want to make a reverse charge phone call, please," she said, breathing shallowly in order to avoid the sour smell.

Rosie's mum wouldn't mind accepting the call. She needed to talk to Rosie. Her mum was going to leave her dad, it was clear now. She said she was going to Greenford. She gave the operator the number and waited.

In her head she kept hearing her dad, his voice hard and brittle *You think you're a girl again . . .*

Her dad would be on his own. She would have to live with one of them and go and visit the other one at weekends.

I'm thirty-six not sixty-six. I just want a bit of frigging life.

What did she mean, "life"?

Rosie would know what to do. Her bitterness, her hurt, tumbled like a tower of toy bricks. Maybe she could go over to Rosie's house and stay the night.

She could hear the operator speaking to someone and then, much louder,

"Caller, you're through."

"Rosie?" she said, her voice starting to clog up. Now that she was about to unburden it all, she was going to cry like a kid.

"Is that you, Annie?" It was Mrs Kelly. "Our Rosie's away to Patricia's. I'll get her to call you. I've said she's to be back by nine-thirty."

In the background Ann could hear the sound of a crying child and beyond that, further away, the theme tune of "Coronation Street".

"No, it's all right." she said and put the phone down. She sat down on the wall of a small flower bed beside the phone box.

She hadn't thanked Mrs Kelly for the reverse charge phone call. She hadn't thought through the date with Tony Kelly. She hadn't checked whether she had a clean ironed shirt for the next day.

She had the beginnings of a ladder in her tights, near her ankle. With her fingers she pulled at the nylon fabric and watched the ladder climb up the side of her leg.

CHAPTER FOURTEEN

Just after break time at school, Ann decided not to go and see Tony Kelly. Somewhere inside her was a sudden revulsion for him that she couldn't explain.

He was the same boy that she'd liked for months. The boy who'd kissed her at the Excelsior, the boy who'd been nice to her whenever she was with Rosie. The boy who'd rowed with Patricia and had asked her out instead.

She looked across the classroom during a French lesson and saw Rosie writing something in her book, her arm crooked round it as though it were a deep secret. A lead weight sank to the bottom of her stomach and she lowered her head and looked at her textbook.

What was her mum doing?

Was she preparing to leave them? Ann shook her head slowly and in doing so caught the eye of the teacher. She looked away and bent closer to her text book.

Was she licking a long piece of cotton and then

with one eye closed stabbing it through the needle of her sewing machine? Ann pictured her creamy skin, her arched eyebrows, her button earrings.

Was she thundering down a seam, not even slowing up near a curve or a bend, her foot pressed hard down, her teeth closed in concentration? In her mind Ann could see the red lipstick, the pink pearls round her neck.

Was she kneeling down, brandishing a long, sharp pair of scissors which took clean bites from a piece of fabric that was spreadeagled on the floor? She imagined her mum, arms outstretched, holding up the cut material, the cream tissue paper still pinned to one side, her gold wedding ring glinting, her long red fingernails shining like glass beads.

Ann held these pictures in her mind, her eyes closed in concentration. Anything was better than the picture of her mum folding up her knickers and bras and petticoats and placing them in the corner of a suitcase.

Anything was better than that.

Rosie and Patricia and her mum and Dermot. They were now linked in her mind as though one situation was a mirror reflection of the other. Somewhere outside, away from the mirror, stood her dad, awkward, grubby and overweight, and there beside him was a small girl in a white nylon dress with a black velvet bolero, her hair frizzed, in her hand a small pouch bag made from the same material as the dress. Ann rubbed her eyes to wipe out the pictures.

She couldn't go to see Tony Kelly that afternoon.

How could she? Going to see him was like trying to grab a bit of fun in the middle of all the misery she felt, like someone walking into the middle of a road accident and trying to buy an ice cream.

Ann slipped out of the side gate while everyone else was making their way to Art. As she went, she saw Rosie twenty yards or so in front, unconcerned, a bounce in her step.

Feeling dismal, she looked to see if any buses were coming and started the walk home.

She'd talk to her mum. She'd tell her everything. The day she saw her at Wood Green with Dermot. Then the Excelsior, her and Dermot dancing and leaving poor Dad on the side holding the drinks.

She walked down Spring Hill, past the flats, past the church and down towards the railway bridge. She'd taken her tie off and undone her shirt buttons because of the heat.

She'd talk to her mum about the happy times they had together as a family when they still lived in the flats. When her dad had had a win at the betting shop and had given them money to buy new things and they'd rushed up to the market at quarter to five to catch the stalls before they closed.

That had been when her mum still worked in Jacksons, before the rows started.

At the pedestrian crossing she helped a woman down the kerb with a big black pram in which there were three small, sticky-looking children.

She was sure they'd been happy in the flats. She remembered her mum buying aftershave for her dad out of her wages and her dad saying "Holy Moses' and dabbing it behind his ears as though he was a woman and it was a bottle of perfume.

She was positive they'd had good times. She watched the woman with the pram move sluggishly up the road. She wondered why her mum had never had another baby. That always seemed to make people happy.

She thought of the weekend computer course that her mum had wanted to go on just before she'd stopped working in the betting shop. Ann hadn't been there when her mum and dad had had the row about it, but she'd come home afterwards and found her crying in the living room, her sewing machine on its side, her material and patterns scattered across the room, the floor littered with hundreds of glinting pins.

Ann had never understood why her dad had been so dead set against it.

She turned into her street feeling apprehensive. There was a removals van at one of the houses near the top. Maybe someone would move in who her mum could make friends with, somebody like blonde Nell or Lil from the flats.

She had to stand for a minute or so as a sofa and some wooden chairs were carried past.

She could be better herself. She could be nicer, less temperamental, spend some more time with her mum. Maybe some of it was her fault. She could change. It wasn't as if she had Rosie to worry about now.

Her way cleared, Ann walked across the street looking down towards her house.

She'd done the right thing to come home early. It would have been terrible to leave it to four o'clock. What if she'd got back from Tony Kelly's and found her mum gone and a note on the mantelpiece?

It was then that she stopped walking and stood frowning. Outside her own house she could see the familiar blue of Dermot's car.

Her strides changed into pigeon steps as she moved slowly forward. What was he doing there?

She took a deep breath and stood on the pavement not knowing what to do. Should she go on or turn round and walk away?

About three doors away from her house she heard their voices. She ducked in behind some dense bushes in a neighbour's garden.

Her mother was laughing. In the distance she heard Dermot saying, "I'm telling you, gerl, it's a long way."

"It's hardly the end of the earth."

Ann held her breath. What were they talking about?

"And me a married man! Can you see it?" Dermot said, laughing.

Her mum and Dermot were getting in the car and Ann peeped out from behind the bush. Her mother had her good cream dress on and red shoes and earrings. Dermot opened the car door for her and then he picked something up from the pavement. It was a suitcase. Her mum and dad's old brown suitcase.

"I'll just put this in the boot," she heard him say. "It weighs a ton!" He had a wide smile on his face and he was dressed up in a suit of some sort. Ann moved back into the garden, her face pressed into the sharp, dry shoots of the bush, her head buzzing.

Her mum was leaving. He was going with her. She was going to Our Mary's first and then they were going to go away together and after the divorce they were going to get married,

And me a married man. Can you see it? he'd said.

Somewhere in the back of her head she heard the car doors slam, the engine start up and the car pull away from the kerb.

Her mum was gone.

She pushed her face into her hands and waited for the tears but they didn't come.

Her mum was gone. She had taken the brown suitcase, the one with the broken lock that had to be fastened with an old belt.

And what was her dad doing now, at this moment? Probably standing in the middle of a dusty building site, a yellow safety helmet on his head, his arms outstretched, holding the construction plans up and looking at the steel that he had erected, rusty and incomprehensible, like the skeleton of some giant prehistoric creature.

She took her hands away from her eyes and looked into the heat of the afternoon. The men were still moving cupboards and rolls of carpet into the house up the road. One of them was leaning on a sideboard in the middle of the pavement. He looked sweaty and tired. It was probably how her dad looked. How much worse he would look when he knew.

Shaking her head in disbelief, she walked off up the road.

CHAPTER FIFTEEN

Tony Kelly opened the door and said,

"Ann. You're here." He sounded surprised. From behind him she could hear the sounds of reggae music.

"Do you want a cold drink? What's the matter?" he said.

She told him there was nothing the matter. She told him that she was just hot and tired after waiting for the bus. She told him exactly how she'd bunked off school and how no one had seen her. She laughed as she said it because she was feeling good.

He gave her a drink of orange, which wasn't all that cold, and she told him about how she liked his house, and how she wasn't only saying that to please him because she actually liked living down the flats better than in the house where she was. She told him about her mates from the flats whom she didn't see any more.

He didn't have a shirt on, just jeans and a gold

cross hanging on a chain round his neck. Her neck felt hot and wet to touch but he looked creamy and cool.

She told him about the new clothes she'd bought and about how she'd planned to buy a new jacket in the autumn.

He didn't say much, didn't look all that happy in fact, but that was all right because she felt like talking, she felt happy.

For no reason at all she explained about the day, many years before, when she'd gone to Southend with her mum and dad and how they'd all walked out onto the sea bed when the tide had gone out. She remembered that it had looked like a huge brown desert. It was slimy to walk on, and every time she'd placed her foot down it felt as though the whole surface of the sea bed was moving slightly. After a while, her dad had started to pick up handfuls of the mud and had thrown it at her or her mum. In their turn, they'd picked up the stuff, too, and begun flinging it at him. The three of them were running and laughing wildly and throwing mud until her dad suddenly looked stern and had told them that that was enough, that you could go too far with games and that a joke was a frigging joke.

She described how they'd walked in silence for a few seconds, her and her mum thinking that her dad was really upset when she'd felt a great big wet lump of mud on the back of her neck and her mum squealed because her dad had stuffed some of the slime down the back of her swimming costume.

After a while they'd got to the sea. Ann had

expected it to be deep so far out but it was just like it was at the shore, shallow and frothy. They'd walked out until it was waist high and washed off the mud and the grime and then suddenly, her dad had looked around with apprehension and had whispered that he could feel the tide turning, that it was starting to come back in, that they'd never get back to the shore in time because the waves would overtake them.

She'd looked towards the shore, which had seemed miles away, the people on it like tiny characters in a film. She'd looked back at the sea and then back to the shore again, her head turning as though it was on a swivel.

Her dad's face had been grim for a minute but after he'd shrugged his shoulders pathetically and looked at her panic-stricken face he'd burst into laughter. She'd realized then that it was a joke and had laughed and punched him in the stomach; she'd pointed to the dark brown water moving back and forth across her feet and laughed again as though the joke lay there somewhere underneath the sea.

They'd walked the long way back, laughing and joking, and although she felt safe holding her parents' hands, every now and then she'd looked round to check that the tide hadn't suddenly taken to a gallop and was pursuing them.

She asked Tony for another drink and if he had anything stronger but he just shook his head. He started to speak a couple of times but stopped and just continued to pour out her drink.

There was a brief silence for a moment and she

started to tell him about her mum and dad and Rosie and Patricia but she'd got muddled and as soon as she'd said "Patricia" he sat up a bit and said, "Ann, about Pat . . ."

But she just shook her head and told him not to talk to her about any of them, that she'd had quite enough of them and didn't want to hear another mention of their names again that afternoon.

After another silence she asked him why they didn't take themselves off up to his bedroom to listen to some records.

He shrugged his shoulders and walked on up the stairs.

She told him to cheer up and that they only had one life and, following him up, she had a kind of regal smile on her face as though she were acknowledging the stairs, the carpet, the towels that hung untidily over the banister.

She took her shoes off and put her feet up on the bed and patted the space that was left beside her. After he'd put a record on he sat down, his legs hanging off the side of the bed, his arm touching hers, stiff and hard.

With her hand she rubbed his arm up and down, up and down.

She told him how glad she was that he'd invited her over. How much she liked him. She was looking down at the bedspread and not at him.

"Look," he started, but she carried on and said that it didn't matter that she couldn't be his real girlfriend, she was just glad that he liked her.

She was quiet for a minute and his arm seemed to have softened as though her rubbing had loosened the muscles. She looked up at the bookshelves opposite and saw the grubby spines of some of the books she'd borrowed.

She asked him if he'd read them all and then said, "They're better than school books, Rosie."

He looked her straight in the face and she realized what she'd done. She'd called him Rosie, as though it was Rosie she thought she was with, not her brother, not Tony Kelly.

"Ann, what's the matter?" he said, his face serious, not like the Tony she knew, the Tony that had been in her head.

The hand that was rubbing his arm began to tremble slightly and in her head her thoughts seemed to playing a game of tag.

You called him Rosie. He thinks you're odd. He thinks you're gone in the head. He's not keen, anyroad. He's regretted asking you. You shouldn't have come, you shouldn't have come.

She put her arms round him and although her eyes were dry and she wasn't sobbing, somewhere inside her head there was a miniature-sized Ann who was lying face down on the floor, her arms and legs kicking in temper, her eyes streaming and her face blotched.

He tried to pull back slightly and said, "Ann, things are not the same . . ."

He was right. Things were not the same now as they had been before, but before he could say any more, Ann pulled him over on top of her and began to kiss him on the mouth, clumsily at first, like a baby sucking eagerly for its food and then more competently. She felt his arms and shoulders relax and after a minute or so he rolled over and lay on top of her.

The record had stopped playing and Ann was just lying on her back on the bed. She felt uncomfortable, her clothes twisted and awkward underneath her. She watched the doorway, waiting for Tony to come back from the bathroom. His jeans lay carelessly on the floor at the side of the bed.

In her head she kept seeing the tiny girl walking back along the dark brown seabed, an adult in each hand, anxiously looking back to search out for the brown frothy waves in the distance.

Her thoughts were broken by the sound of the toilet flushing and she sat up trying to straighten her clothes. She noticed that the button had come off the waist of her skirt and saw it in the fold of the bedspread. Beside her, just under her elbow, were her tights, deflated and crumpled.

She hoped he'd be smiling when he walked back through the door, that he'd come over and hug her, kiss her (maybe even tell her he loved her). Wasn't that what happened in films and books?

Instead he looked away from her when he walked in the door and began to put his jeans on.

"I'll have to tidy up in a minute," he said.

"Oh," was all she could say. He wanted her to go.

"Look, Annie," he started. He was calling her "Annie" again.

"That's a nice cross," she said. She didn't want a serious conversation. She didn't want him talking to her in a sensible way, not after what had just happened.

"Pat gave it me," he said, sitting on the side of the bed.

He'd been seeing Patricia. He and Patricia had been together.

"Are you back together?"

"Not really. I don't know. Maybe." Tony and Patricia were going back together again. He knew that, when she arrived. He knew that, when they went to his bedroom. He knew that, when her button snapped off and her tights were discarded.

"I tried to talk to you about it, but you were . . . so . . . so . . . preoccupied."

Ann lifted her feet off the bed. She picked up her clothes and her shoes and walked past Tony Kelly, out into the hall and into the bathroom. She closed the door and shot the lock. After standing still in the middle of the tiny room she pulled down the lid of the toilet seat and sat on it.

Had he tried to talk to her about it? All she could remember was a torrent of words that mostly came from her. Would it have made any difference if he had? Wouldn't she still have put her head back on his pillow and helped undo buttons on things that he couldn't manage?

She started to put her feet into her tights but her legs were damp and clammy and the nylon fabric kept sticking.

She looked at her watch. It said two thirty-five. She held it up to her ear; she was sure it was later, positive she had been here hours. But it was only twenty-five to three. She'd arrived at about ten to two.

She'd only been with Tony Kelly for forty-five minutes. It seemed like hours.

Pulling her tights up to her waist, she looked in the mirror. The skin on her face was red where it had rubbed against his face. Her hair was sticking up at the back. She put the plug in the sink and filled it with cold water. She gasped as she dipped her face in and with her hands she splashed her hair and the back of her neck.

She looked at her watch again, it was two thirty-eight. There was no point in going home. There would be nobody there, at least until her dad came.

She felt a stab of anguish as she pictured her dad, standing looking into her mum's wardrobe, the silver hangers swinging to and fro inside, the plastic bag that used to cover the cream dress hanging like a dismal ghost.

Perhaps he already knew. Perhaps he was there now, waiting for her. She couldn't go back there yet. She couldn't face him.

Her legs felt sticky against her tights and she sat on the side of the bath and thought about what she would do.

"Are you all right, Annie?" She heard Tony Kelly's voice from outside the door. He sounded tentative, worried. He had gone back to calling her "Annie" again. She was his sister's mate again. Round his neck was a gold cross from his proper girlfriend.

She opened the bathroom door and walked past him, down the stairs and out of the house.

He didn't follow her.

165

PART FOUR

Decisions

Maureen O'Brien held the plastic roller in her hand
and reached for the tiny rectangle of tissue paper.
She expertly covered the wet hair with it and curled
it up into the roller. Ann could smell the perm
lotion and feel the curlers pulling at the very roots
of her hair.

"Mum, you're rolling up my skin as well!" she
said.

"Give over," her mother said, holding her wet
hair at right angles to her head. She began to hum
a song, and Ann sat back in the chair bracing herself
for the next bit of pain that the process would incur.

It was all part of a new leaf her mother was
turning over for her.

"You're so dowdy looking. You've got to pick
yourself up. I know you've been upset . . ." Her
mother rarely mentioned the accident. "You've got
to pull yourself together. There'll be other pals and

166

boys too. It'll not be long until you're going out on dates. And there's the wedding in December to look forward to!"

They'd reached a kind of compromise. She was going to let her mother do her hair provided she had some shop-bought clothes, from the shop of her choice (not Marks & Spencer's).

It had been the letter from Dermot that had started it all off. It was short and to the point and she had read it so often that she could almost remember it off by heart.

Dear John and Maureen,

I hope you're both well Geraldine is well out of hospital now I've decided to stay and the wedding is on 9th December in St Johns in West Dublin You're all invited I can't stay a single man all my life worse luck. Love
Dermot Duffy
PS Love to Ann.

He was to be married in December and they were all invited. Her mum had seemed delighted and had immediately started to sort through her pile of magazines and dress patterns. Ann had looked at the letter with suspicion but had allowed herself to be carried along with the plans. The car on the ferry; a long weekend trip; a bit of sight-seeing round Dublin; some Christmas shopping; a trip up to Oxford Street for a wedding gift.

The flutter over plans took her mind off other things. It took her mind off the telegram Dermot must have got from Ireland to say his fiancée had appendicitis. It meant that she didn't dwell on the journey he must have made round to her mum's that day (the day of the accident) to borrow the brown suitcase. Perhaps he'd brought his clothes with him in a carrier bag and then her mum had packed them for him and fastened the suitcase with an old brown leather belt.

She'd been wrong about her mum leaving them. Had she been wrong about the other things? She'd seen them at the Wood Green, together. She'd seen them kissing at the Excelsior; hadn't she?

It was all so long ago.

She held the towel tightly up round her forehead while her mum squirted the cold neutraliser over the curlers on her head. She shivered as it ran over her scalp and then trickled out onto her skin.

"Mum!" she said.

"Give over!" Her mum's voice was disdainful and she seemed to squirt it all the harder.

Afterwards, she sat looking in the mirror for a while. Her hair did look better, there was no doubt. It looked fuller, as though she had twice as much hair as she actually had. Her mum had used a weaker perm so there was no frizz.

For a moment she imagined herself with a matching skirt and top and boots, a bag hanging loosely over her shoulder. She saw herself walking with her parents into the reception of Dermot's wedding, taking small glasses of sherry as they passed the waitresses.

Then she turned away from the mirror and shook her head with bitterness. It had all turned out all right for them. Her mum and dad seemed happy. Dermot was getting married. Tony and Patricia were back together again.

But it had not turned out all right for Rosie.

And as she ticked the dates off in her school diary she knew that it was not going to turn out all right for her.

Some days later she sat on the armchair in the front room, her hair gently flicking round her ears, a new skirt and jumper hanging in her wardrobe and looked sadly at her parents as they sat huddled down one end of the settee, the ferry brochures spread out in front of them.

There would be no trip to Dublin for her.

It was Sunday but Kate Martin wasn't getting ready to go to mass. It was ten o'clock and her jacket was still under a plastic bag in the wardrobe.

She was sitting on a chair in her living room. In her hand she had two letters. The top one was from Rose Kelly's father.

Dear Miss Martin,

Thank you for coming to see us last Tuesday evening. It is a great comfort to Mrs Kelly and I to see how many friends we have at a time like this. Mrs Kelly attends mass daily and prays for dear Rose. She is always in our thoughts.

We were sorry to hear that Ann O'Brien is so poorly. Mrs Kelly thinks it's just that she's missing Rose – as we all are – and that she'll get over it in a short while. It's a shame she doesn't have brothers and sisters herself. It would take her mind off Rose and the terrible accident.

We thought hard about what you said about the accident itself and in the end we couldn't see that it was any more than that – an accident. It's true that Rose was a big "sensible" girl but perhaps there was just a thoughtless moment when she stepped out into the road. Perhaps Ann O'Brien is just upset because she actually saw the lorry hit Rose. Who knows what pictures there are in her mind. We didn't talk about it for long though, Mrs Kelly gets too upset, you understand.

The man who drove the lorry has been to see us, you know, he came again yesterday, said he'd just been passing. He started to talk about summer holidays and then was embarrassed, lost for words. We don't feel bitter towards him. It's affected his life deeply. At least he doesn't cry when he comes now. Mrs Kelly told him, there was nothing he could have done, it was all part of God's plan.

There's a Novena at the church in November, so Sister Dominic says. I hope we see you there.

Yours sincerely
Michael Kelly

Kate put the letter down and sat back in her armchair. God's plan. It was all part of God's plan. She let the letter drop out of her hand onto her lap.

She'd been teaching all day on the day that Rose Kelly got killed. She'd been busy, irritable; she'd snapped at girls as they lounged round the corridors and kept some in at lunchtime for not doing homework. At least it hadn't been Rose. At least her last encounter with Rose hadn't been awful.

Had Rose been friendly with her mother, when she'd left home that last morning? She thought of Rose lying on the ground, her shoe a few feet away from her. Had her mother told her off about the shoes, told her to wear another pair because those kind – with pointed heels – weren't allowed? Kate imagined Mrs Kelly looking up the street after her daughter with exasperation, nodding her head, resolving to get her husband to speak to the girl.

And then she hadn't come home, and all Mrs Kelly had seen was two dark blue uniforms throwing their silhouettes on her front door.

It was God's plan. It was all part of God's plan. Kate picked up the other letter. It was from Sister Dominic.

Dear Kate,

Mrs O'Brien rang me up last week and said that you had been round to see her. I also heard through Father Peter that you have been to see Mr and Mrs Kelly.

While I am happy that you have taken it on yourself to console these bereaved people I am extremely unhappy that you have continued to talk about the death of Rose Kelly as though it were a great mystery.

The police's view is that it was an accident. The coroner's view was the same. It is only upsetting the parents of each of the girls that you are insisting that it was not.

I am particularly distressed that you have gone ahead in this endeavour even after we talked about it.

I think we need to meet. I note that you are free on Monday after recess. I shall be in my office.

Yours sincerely
Sister Dominic

Kate knew what Sister Dominic would say. We are not meant to understand these things, Kate. It's hard to accept, but if we have faith we must believe that God has his reasons.

God has his reasons. In spite of herself, she saw God as a Father Christmas character who went round giving to his people. Rose Kelly was given to her parents. They loved her, cared for her, had plans for her future. But then God took her back again because he had other plans.

Kate shook her head again.

These were childish thoughts, unworthy of a thirty-year-old Catholic. There were all sorts of mysteries about faith. She had never questioned them before. Everybody said it was an accident. It wasn't her place to insist.

She ought to let the whole thing drop.

The telephone rang suddenly and she was startled out of her thoughts.

"Yes?" she said forgetting to say her number.

"Is that Miss Martin?" The voice was faltering, nervous. Kate knew immediately who it was.

"Miss Martin, it's Ann O'Brien. I'm sorry to bother you. You said I could call."

"Yes, of course." Kate looked at the letter in her hand from Sister Dominic.

"Could I come and see you. Today?"

"I don't know . . ." She was seeing Sister Dominic in the morning. If she saw Ann she'd have to admit that she had yet again ignored her advice.

"Don't worry then. It's not important." The girl's voice was trailing off. She was losing her.

"Come for tea," Kate quickly said, in a bright voice. "I'm making a sponge."

She put the phone down and folded the letters up and pushed them into a drawer in the sideboard. She looked at her watch. It was twenty to eleven. If she hurried she could just get to eleven o'clock mass.

Instead, she went into her kitchen, got out a cookery book and began to flick through. She began to hum and after a few seconds lay the book open on the page for Victoria Sponge Cake.

CHAPTER SIXTEEN

Tony Kelly hadn't followed her and there was a growing sense of apprehension inside her as she walked towards the bus stop. Even though she knew in her heart that he would not come after her, she still looked back two or three times as she walked along. The empty street behind her heightened the sense of dread that was filling her inside. Once at the bus stop she made her decision. She'd go back to school and see Rosie. Rosie would know what to do.

Ann sat upstairs on the bus back to school. The heat was overpowering and she picked up a discarded newspaper and began to fan herself. If the traffic wasn't too heavy, she'd be there in time to meet Rosie.

What have you done? What have you done? A voice in her head seemed to say.

She ignored it and kept looking out of the window. She thought for a minute that she could see Dermot's car driving past, metallic blue, her mother's knees neatly crossed in the front seat, but when it passed and overtook the bus she could see the back of an old man's head and another man in the passenger seat.

She kept looking down at her legs and fancying that she could see wrinkles in the tights from where they had been crumpled up underneath her, as though they might give her away. But everybody knew that tights didn't crease; tights just bounced back into shape whatever happened to them.

Why was she thinking about tights? After what she had done?

Her stomach seemed to crumple for a moment as she thought of Tony Kelly lying across the bed, his head buried in her neck, his body tense and then suddenly relaxed.

What have you done?

She saw her dad's face that afternoon picking a letter from the mantelpiece, reading her mum's excuses, disbelieving at first, then angry. "Holy Moses", he might say, or "frig me". Perhaps he wouldn't be surprised, perhaps he already knew. Maybe she was the one who was supposed to have gone home and found a note. Maybe there in the middle of her dressing table was a small white envelope with "Ann" written on it, her dad shuffling about in the hall, feeling sorry for her instead of the other way round.

For a moment she felt righteous. No one could blame her for what happened this afternoon. She had been driven to it. She'd needed someone to talk to. Tony had been her friend.

But Tony Kelly wasn't her friend. She hardly knew him. He was Rosie's brother, Patricia's boyfriend. He had been pleasant to her, he had asked her to dance and kissed her (in front of Patricia). He had even asked her round on a sort of date.

She started to tap her fingers lightly on the back of the seat in front and felt the painfully slow pull of the bus as it seemed to drag itself away from stops and back out into the traffic. In the heat, all the cars seemed to be slowing down and making loud wheezing noises as they crept up hills and eased away from traffic lights. She found herself taking shallow breaths and fanning herself frantically as though everything depended on her keeping cool.

A couple of older men were sitting up the front blowing smoke rings and looking at newspapers. One man had a small pencil behind his ear and every now and again he swapped it with his cigarette while he marked off something on the newspaper.

It was his betting pencil. Her dad had dozens of them at home. They were usually short and always looked as though they needed sharpening. She remembered that she had done it once; she'd collected all her dad's pencils from his trouser pockets, the dashboard of his car, the area of floor beside his armchair and patiently inserted each one into her sharpener until the end of it was like a needle. He'd laughed and given her a hug but she'd known he hadn't been pleased. She'd heard him tell her mum that they stuck in his legs through his trouser pockets and if he turned a corner quick the one behind his ear was liable to impale his eye.

She'd laughed at the time because it hadn't been important. It had only been a pile of pencils. But now she felt on the edge of tears. I try to do my best for them, she thought, self pity creeping out of the corners of her eyes and filling her nose up.

Then, just as quickly as she started, she stopped. She wiped her nose and eyes on a tiny square of green tissue and went to put it back in her pocket, but it was sopping wet so she dropped it on the floor by her feet.

That's why it had happened this afternoon. It would serve them all right. She had been pushed to the edge. It wasn't her fault. Her mum had left them.

But did you have to sleep with him? For a moment she saw her mum's disappointed face and heard her voice.

I didn't sleep with him she would say, seeing a beautiful couple lying side by side in a bed of silk sheets, the man with his naked arm draped over the woman, their eyes shut, their breathing steady.

"Well, what do you call it then?" her mother's voice persisted.

It wasn't really sleeping or making love, it was just a muck around. Nothing really happened.

But her legs had felt sticky afterwards and he hadn't looked her in the face. Where was he now? Had he gone up to St John's? Was he leaning against the gate waiting for his friends to swagger out?

He'll be boasting about it to everyone. Your name'll be ruined, her mother said in a sharp whisper, some anger coming into her voice.

Well, what about you and Dermot? she wanted to shout back. What about your goings on? What about my poor dad?

Yes, what about your poor dad? When he finds this out — and he will, word gets round — what will he feel? His little girl.

She closed her eyes and held them shut.

What have I done?

They hadn't really done anything, just messed around. He'd touched her and they'd kissed and he'd pulled about with her clothes. She hadn't said No. She hadn't said anything, because nothing had seemed to matter.

It was all right though, because you were meant to feel a great pain when it happened and she hadn't felt anything.

But her legs had been sticky afterwards and he was probably talking about her to the boys outside the school gates at that very minute — and Patricia had got him back. She was his real girlfriend.

The bus was moving into Enfield Mount and she was due to get off in a couple of stops. She looked at her watch. She would just be in time for the final bell. Would Rosie speak to her? What if Patricia was there?

Of course she would speak to her. They had only had a squabble. Rosie would know what to do. She would probably laugh it off when she told her and say "That's nothing" or "So what! Everyone does that, Patricia told me."

That's what would happen. She would make up

with Rosie and Rosie would reassure her, calm her down.

"What?" Rosie looked at her, shocked. "In our house? Just now?"

"But that's not the worst," Ann said, trying to dwarf her confession with bigger problems. "My mum's gone. She's left with Dermot. I saw them driving off."

Rosie shrugged her shoulders and leaned back against the wall. She was cold, there had been no pleasure in her face when Ann had walked up, no delight when Ann had said, "Look, I need to talk to you."

"When did all this – you and him – when did that start?"

It's not important! she wanted to say, my mum's gone!

She leaned back against the wall as well. This hadn't happened the way she'd hoped, not at all. She'd wanted Rosie to welcome her with open arms. But Rosie didn't seem bothered. The thing that had really taken her aback was about her and Tony, because that was the bit that affected her other friend – Patricia.

Ann was angry. All these people were only interested in the bits of her life that affected their own. None of them cared about the whole of her. She felt the dread in her stomach for a moment and in her head there was nausea. What she needed was a good illness where she was lying in a bed and everybody was standing round worried about her.

"What about Pat? Did he say anything about Pat?"

That was all she cared about now, now that she was Patricia's friend and not hers.

"Sod. you. Sod you all," Ann said. She walked off up the road and turned quickly to cross not knowing quite where she was going. In the back of her mind she could hear the click of Rosie's heels as she followed her. She put her foot off the pavement and walked boldly forward and a small blue van whizzed by, almost touching her. She felt the blast as the breeze in its wake hit her amid the heavy afternoon heat and stood, statue-like with shock, at the side of the road.

She saw herself in a hospital bed with tubes and charts around her, doctors writing notes on clipboards and a nurse saying, don't talk for too long, she's very weak. Her mother and father would be there, shocked at her accident.

"Watch it," Rosie said, her voice anxious. Ann looked hopefully round but Rosie's expression rapidly changed; she averted her eyes and in a harsh voice said, "It's not worth getting killed for."

Rosie didn't care for her any more. She was a nuisance to her.

"Isn't it?" Ann said, looking back at the road. If she had just stepped out in front of the van . . .

She pictured herself with one leg in mid air, losing her balance in the path of the van like someone on a tightrope who was about to fall off.

If she were to wait until a slow car were coming by, step out in time for the driver to see her and put the brakes on – it would only be a tap, a concussion, some bruises, a broken rib or a broken arm. There'd be an ambulance and a few weeks off school. Her mum would come back; it would pull them back to their senses. Rosie – well, that was up to her.

"You're so stupid," Rosie said dismissively. She was looking at her watch. She was probably meeting Patricia and Ann was keeping her back.

In the distance there was a small mini coming towards them. If she just had the courage to step off the pavement.

"You go on. Don't worry about me. I wouldn't want you to be late." The mini was coming closer.

Rosie looked towards the mini and then back to Ann. "For God's sake, you're nuts. This isn't going to do anything." Rosie walked across and put her arm out. Ann shook the arm off and Rosie had a look of incomprehension on her face.

"You mean it, don't you?" Rosie said. She actually thought she meant to do it. Ann almost smiled, almost wanted to laugh. Let her think it. Rosie had dropped her, let her worry.

Ann turned back to the road and tried to step out, but Rosie had dropped her school bag on the pavement and had somehow grabbed her by the hand, holding her back. Rosie's face had softened. She looked for a moment like the old Rosie, her friend. Ann's pull relaxed and Rosie grabbed her other hand. Maybe the threat was enough. If she just stepped back onto the pavement, they could go on as they had been before.

Her mum would never know, though. Her mum wouldn't come back.

The mini was almost up to them and she tried to snatch her hands away, but Rosie was pulling her back, "Get off," she said, her temper rising but it was too late. The car had passed slowly by and she had lost her chance. She pulled again with anger and Rosie's face was grim, looking at her and then at the cars and then back at her. There were parked cars, but they weren't close enough to make a difference to her view and Ann kept looking up the road to see what was coming.

Rosie's grip was like a vice and Ann pulled away, more from temper than determination. They were moving backwards and forwards as though they were two kids in a playground pulling in a tug of war.

Rosie was pulled onto the road. "Grow up!" she said and with a huge determined tug she pulled both of them back onto the pavement.

She hadn't changed at all. In a frenzy of frustration, Ann tried to pull one hand out and then the other, forcing them to revolve slowly until Rosie was on the outside and she was closest to the gardens.

"Ann, stop it!" Rosie said.

"Let me go!" Ann said it with rage. She began to pull her hands furiously and the two girls started turning in a slow circle, Ann all the time trying to steer herself back off the pavement, and Rosie holding stubbornly on. It was as though they were having a strange game of Ring-a-Ring-o'-Roses. Rosie's face was crimson with heat and Ann was feeling sweat forming on her back and under her arms.

They turned and turned and afterwards Ann would remember the view she had had behind Rosie's head of the cars, the trees, the school, the cars, the trees, the school, the cars, the trees, the school.

Then Rosie let go.

Suddenly she seemed to catapult away from Ann. Ann tried to stop the turning but was dizzied. She heard the trundle of the lorry's wheels; she heard the screech of the brakes and she was still steadying herself, unconsciously rubbing her hands where Rosie's grip had made them sore.

She looked round for Rosie, across the road, behind her. She saw her school bag sitting by the edge of the pavement. She saw the great lorry stopped in the distance and from behind it the driver running towards her.

He was probably annoyed at the both of them fighting, giving him a jump, making him stop unnecessarily because he thought they would tumble into the pathway of his lorry.

And then she saw Rosie lying on the road, her arms and legs splayed out as though she was trying to touch the four corners of her bed. One of her shoes was lying on the road a couple of yards away.

The driver was crying.

She probably had a hanky. She looked through her pockets. I haven't got one, she thought she said. She walked closer. Rosie's skirt was hitched up one side, her pants were almost showing. She bent over and pulled it down and in the background there were voices of people coming closer.

Rosie's leg was warm. There'd be an ambulance soon. She walked over and picked up Rosie's shoe. If she didn't pick it up then no one would and Rosie wouldn't be able to wear them again.

She stood by the side of the road and watched as the crowd of girls and people stood around looking at the still girl on the tarmac. A nun and a teacher pushed through and ran into the middle of the circle.

She'd hold onto the shoe anyway. She could at least do that.

PART FIVE

The Truth

"Sister Dominic has a parent in there, Kate. She'll only be a minute. Would you mind waiting?"

Kate sat down in one of the soft chairs in the waiting area outside Sister Dominic's office. She felt at ease. Her qualms at seeing the headmistress had dissipated during her talk with Ann O'Brien. She was looking forward to clearing the whole matter up. Sister Dominic would say to her "It was an accident" and she would be able to agree because that was what it had been – an accident.

She sat back in her chair and remembered her talk with Ann O'Brien with some satisfaction. The girl had been in a terrible state and had taken ages to tell her story. She had looked away from Kate as she'd unfolded the events of the afternoon. She'd made a decision to skip school because she was worried about her mother. Then there had been the journey back to her home and seeing her mother leave with the suitcase and her dad's best friend. She had stared into some point on Kate's carpet as she described the events.

She'd hung around in a local park for an hour or so, not knowing what to do, and then made her way back to school to see Rosie, her best friend.

Kate had had to go across and sit with her at this point as her words came falteringly through shudders and sobs. Kate's sponge cake had sat uneaten on the coffee table.

Inside, Kate had felt a great elation. She had been right. There had been more to the accident than everybody thought. She had been patient and now she was being rewarded with the truth.

Ann O'Brien had decided to get run over in order to bring her mother back. Rosie had been against it and had tried to physically stop her, but in the confusion and struggle it had been Rosie who'd got thrown onto the road in front of the lorry that neither of them had noticed.

After these words had spilled out, Ann O'Brien calmed down. Her face was less red and her words less confused.

Kate had spoken quietly and soberly. Ann had not intended Rosie to be hurt in any way. It really had been an accident; not the accident that the coroner and everyone else thought, but an accident all the same.

Kate had driven Ann home. She'd sat strangely quiet in the car but she had stopped crying. She seemed to take deep breaths and Kate imagined she had unloaded a great weight from her shoulders. Kate had told her it wouldn't go any further.

It had taken one great worry from Kate's mind. She had been afraid that Ann would come and tell her some dreadful story that she would feel obliged to tell her parents or Sister Dominic. She had put herself in a silly position. She had promised to keep whatever she was told confidential, and yet there were things that – in her professional role – she couldn't have kept to herself.

But it hadn't mattered. She had spent an hour or so with the girl and let her pour out her story. There was no necessity to inform anyone of the new facts because none of these would change the original verdict. It still would be "Accidental Death". There was nothing to gain by bringing the issue out again.

Sister Dominic's door opened and a young couple came out. Kate stood up, brushing off the fine film of chalk dust which had covered her skirt and smiled at the man and woman.

Inside the office she could see the grim face of Sister Dominic as she shuffled papers and books about on her desk.

Kate had been right to "interfere"; she had been right to offer the girl a shoulder to cry on. It had all worked out for the best. Ann O'Brien would come back to school any day and pick up the pieces of her life. Her story was over.

"Come in, Kate." The headmistress called out from her office.

All she had to do was to pacify Sister Dominic.

* * *

Why did I bother to come all this way? Ann
O'Brien thought as she watched the long line of
traffic inching forward along Wood Green High
Road. She looked through the cars and lorries and
buses to the chemist shop across the road. Come
back in an hour, they'd said.

She'd wanted to have the test done somewhere
where no one could possibly know her. She could
have gone to Finsbury Park or Muswell Hill, instead
she found herself upstairs on a bus heading for
Wood Green.

She sat on a high stool in MacDonald's, a plastic
cup of Coke in her hand, a half-eaten doughnut
resting on a piece of cardboard on the table.

She wondered what was happening in the chemist's
shop to her specimen. Did they look at it under a
microscope or put it into a machine? How could
they tell from that tiny amount of urine what your
body was up to?

She felt jumpy inside and sat up straight in
the chair, as though slouching might somehow
contribute to the sentence the chemist was going
to come out and give her. She'd got dressed up
that morning as well and walked smartly into the
chemist's and said "Please", and "Thank you very
much", as though those things might sway the
chemist one way or another, as though the answer
wasn't really in the specimen but it was all down to
the way the chemist felt.

Her mum hadn't noticed her getting ready because
she'd been dressed up herself to go up to Oxford

Street and get Dermot Duffy's wedding present. She'd been fluttering about in the kitchen, folding up ten pound notes and putting them in the various pockets of her bag and her coat because of the pickpockets. She'd left Ann's school uniform hanging over the banister and kissed her lightly on the forehead before she left. In her bag was a pattern for a two-piece suit from Vogue. Don't be late for school on your first day back, she'd said, and Ann had watched the door close behind her.

Ann broke off a piece of the doughnut and put it into her mouth. She'd stopped feeling sick and her appetite had come back. If Miss Martin knew that, she would probably put it all down to the good "talk" they'd had on the previous Sunday. Adults were funny like that. They liked to think that the good things that happened to you were all part of their doing, their plan, their influence. The bad things were due to you going off the rails in some way, rejecting their advice and turning away from them.

On her way to Miss Martin's flat on the Sunday, she had known she wasn't going to tell the whole story. Standing outside Miss Martin's front door she suddenly wondered why she had bothered to come at all. What was the point of trying to get something "off your chest" if you swallowed huge chunks of it back? She almost turned round and left except that the door had opened and there had been her English teacher standing in her bedroom slippers pulling her gently by the hand inside the door.

It had been an unreal situation, her sitting

opposite a woman whose only connection with her was through verbs and nouns and semi colons; a woman who had made her read poems and books just because these activities were meant to be good for her.

And there she had been, her head full to bursting with parts of speech, ready to link them all in some desperate composition. She'd felt silly and awkward and wished she hadn't come.

But in the end she'd started talking and as the words spilled out her head felt lighter in some indefinable way. It was as though all those sentences, and paragraphs and words had been folded tightly inside her, waiting to be said. She had unpacked them one by one and they had settled somewhere else now. Her head was lighter, easier.

When she said, finally, "It was me that should have gone under that lorry, not Rosie" the words came out in huge capitals and she could imagine them hanging in the air of the room too damning to just fade away like the rest. She'd foolishly looked through the haze of tears to see them there as though there might be a speech bubble suspended somewhere near the light bulb.

That was why she had gone to Miss Martin's; she had wanted to make room inside her head. There were other things she had to think about.

She looked out of the window for a moment at the faces of women edging along the street with their shopping bags and their shoulders rounded. She wondered where her mum was, and for a moment visualized her loitering around the china department in John Lewis or running her fingers along a roll of silk fabric, her forehead wrinkled with mental arithmetic.

Still gazing through the window, she felt a shock of recognition as a face passed behind a parked lorry on the other side of the road. There was a lurch inside her chest and for a moment everything went out of her head. She was no longer in Macdonald's in Wood Green waiting for the results of a test. She was no longer nearly sixteen, friendless, embittered and not sure of what the immediate future would bring.

She was a newcomer to the school and Rosie Kelly came over and gave her a book in a plain brown bag. She was waiting outside a classroom and Rosie Kelly came past and linked her arm and told her the latest joke she had heard. She was walking along Enfield Mount towards Rosie's bus stop singing a song they'd heard on the radio, Rosie doing the main voice and she doing the back up.

She craned her head to look at the person who was walking behind the lorry. In her mind she knew it couldn't be Rosie, she knew that Rosie was dead, but she held her breath and braced herself as the figure appeared at the other end of the lorry.

She could see a chocolate brown jacket edged with yellow. She could see the confident stride of a teenage boy. Beside him was a small dark girl half walking, half running to keep up with him. It was Tony Kelly. Her whole body relaxed and crumpled back into the seat.

It was funny but she'd never noticed any resemblance before. She watched him in a detached way and shook her head. He was completely different from his sister; stocky where Rosie had been thin and angular; dark hair where Rosie had been gingerish. There had been something about the two of them though, the way they held themselves or their expression or the way they both laughed.

The couple were almost out of sight by then and Ann looked at the back of the dark girl who was talking animatedly and fleetingly thought of Patricia.

After a few minutes she looked at her watch. She'd been in Macdonald's for forty minutes. She reached down into her shoulder bag and pulled out a book. It was called *Sins of Yesterday* and on the cover were the words "erotic" and "nail-biting". There was a picture of a woman in a low-cut Regency dress and a cavalier was pointing a pistol at the space between her breasts.

She opened the book about a third of the way in and read for a minute or so. She found her gaze being drawn back to the window, through the traffic jam and into the window of the chemist's shop. She closed the book. She'd found it difficult to get into anyway.

She'd go over and see the chemist early. If it wasn't ready she could wait there. She got up, smoothed down her skirt and jacket and walked out of the doors and in the direction of the chemist's.

When she knew for sure she'd make some plans.

That was the best thing to do.